OF EXILE AND SONG

WANDERERS OF RUIN
BOOK ONE

TIFFANY HUNT

WILD INK PUBLISHING

For those who dream.

ABOUT OF EXILE AND SONG

I've been hunted my whole life.

I am part siren, a hated half-breed. Forced to live in hiding, I use magic to steal and avoid the mages who would punish me for what I am. In a land ravaged by war, it's the only way to survive. The only way to feed my family.

I can change my destiny.

But when tragedy happens and the mages catch up with me, I am badly outnumbered, and if it weren't for the appearance of a stranger, I might have found myself sold to the nearest freak show, or worse. But this mysterious man doesn't help me out of the kindness of his heart. He's after something that could change my family's life forever. And I would be a fool not to help him while I try to steal it for myself.

If only my heart doesn't get in the way.

We form a tentative alliance, and suddenly, my hopes and dreams are within reach. I'll do anything to save my family, and that includes betraying a perfect stranger. So I shouldn't like when Col brushes his hand against mine, or when his voice encourages me to obey. These are only distractions, and I can't afford to forget what's at stake.

But Col has a secret, one that will upend our quest and plunge us into harrowing danger. And I must choose between duty to my family... and duty to my heart.

TRIGGER/CONTENT WARNINGS

Of Exile and Song is set in a medieval style dark fantasy world ruled by a blood-thirsty tyrant, where anyone who is deemed "different" is reviled and subjected to torture, slavery, or death. As a result, the main female character begins the story with ongoing emotional trauma.

Certain other elements might be difficult for some readers, including graphic (consensual) sexual content; graphic violence; references to sexual violence and an attempted sexual assault; past family trauma; death of a friend/person who is disabled; and starvation.

DRAGONLANDS

ORC LANDS

IRONSET

RAVENFELL PASS

IRON DEEP

PRISMVALE

SILVER MINES

GLIMMERDALE

FELL MARSHES

THE
GLIMMERING
SEA

SAMARA'S
VILLAGE

THE DESOLATION

MINES

RUINS

BATTLEFIELD

CHAPTER ONE

"*S*amara," the voice hissed.

I turned over in bed. Cold air whistled through a gap in the slats of the wall, the same hole that had brought the voice. "I'm awake," I whispered back. Nothing else needed to be said, and I quickly stuffed the hole with a rag to ward off the chill.

The bed was pushed up against the wall and took up the entire room, with a sliver of space near the open doorway for a shelf with our clothes. Careful not to wake my sleeping sister, I eased over her. She stirred, and I froze. When her breathing evened out once more, I got out of our shared bed.

Immediately, I missed the warm blankets and hurried to dress. Baggy pants cinched up with a belt, long woolen shirt, and my worn leather boots. I laced the boots tightly so I wouldn't lose one. They were a bit big for my feet, having once belonged to my brother, but they worked well enough.

"What are you doing?"

I turned to see Laney sitting up in bed, her dark eyes reflecting the dim glow of the fire in the next room. Her hair was dark brown like mine, but her eyes were larger than a normal child's, taking up more of her face than they should have. It was just enough to be off-putting for most people.

I adored her eyes, though. "Go back to sleep."

She yawned and stretched. "Why are you sneaking out again?"

"What do you mean, 'sneaking out *again*'?" I asked sternly.

She pouted. "I'm seven years old now. I know things."

I stifled a laugh. Ever since her birthday, Laney had been making similar pronouncements. "What sort of things?" I whispered as I slung my satchel over my shoulder and looked for my knife.

"I know that you sneak out sometimes, and I heard Flint's voice." She pronounced his name as "Vlint" because of her missing front teeth.

"Gods, Laney, I'm not sneaking out with Flint." I *was* sneaking out with Flint, but just for some wholesome thieving. "Go back to sleep. You know too much for a seven-year-old."

"How much are seven-year-olds supposed to know?" She swung her legs out of bed as if she were going with me, and talked so loudly I thought she'd wake our father in the next room. Quickly, I tucked her back into the blankets, making them tight around her body.

"I guess seven-year-olds know what they know," I sighed. "But you don't need to know what I'm doing, and

I need you to stay here and go back to sleep. Keep an eye on Da when you wake up, though."

"I wanna go."

"Not this time. Besides, I'll be back sometime in the morning, and I'll have walked a long way. Too far for your little legs."

"They're not little," she said petulantly.

"Okay then. They're not little, but they are shorter than mine, and that's what I meant."

"But I don't want to look after Da," she whined, switching tactics. "He just sleeps all the time."

"And that's why he needs someone to look after him. Because sleeping people need someone to watch over them."

"Who's going to watch me sleep while *you're* gone?"

It was a practical question, and I saw that I'd laid the trap for myself.

"I will. I'm always watching over you, Laney."

"But you'll be gone!"

"But not for long. Please, will you be a good girl and get your own breakfast in the morning and make Da's special tea when he wakes? He'll need you here. And Rose will be here after she feeds Thomas."

Laney sighed heavily, shook her hair off her face, and looked away. She was a handful, as all children were, but she was a sweet child. If I told her to stay put, she would. I figured that would change in a few years, but for now, I had her wrapped around my finger.

And she did me, as well. I'd do anything for her. Had done many things for her. I grabbed her rag doll and tucked it in next to her.

"Rose doesn't let me play outside like you do," Laney said, picking at a stray thread on the doll.

"That's because it's difficult to watch Baby Thomas and you at the same time." And Rose was just as afraid as I was of Laney being spotted by the wrong people, so she took extra precautions. "You'll be good for her, won't you?"

"Yeah," she whispered, "but I still want to go with you."

"I'll be back in the afternoon. It won't be long."

Resigned to not getting her way, Laney took my hand and gave it a squeeze. I ran my fingers lightly over the webbing between hers, marveling at the delicate green veins that graced her hands. Then I traced a line where skin stopped and scales started.

"That tickles," she giggled.

I shushed her. "Remember to wear your gloves while I'm gone. Don't let anybody in the house."

The two rules Laney lived by. "I won't," she said.

"Promise?"

"Promise."

"Swear it, Laney," I said.

"I swear it," she said solemnly. Then she frowned. "Promise you'll come back?"

My throat closed up, but I kissed her forehead and whispered, "Don't I always?"

Tucking my knife into my boot and pulling a hood over my head, I tiptoed into the only other room of our small, dilapidated house. My father slept on a pallet near the fire, snoring and coughing intermittently. I paused at the door as a coughing fit overtook him. His shoulders shook and there was a rattling sound at the end of each breath. It wasn't good; he would need a poultice when I returned. The fire was still burning and giving warmth to the room, so I grabbed my bow and quiver of arrows and ducked out, shutting the door quietly behind me.

Our father was worse off than Laney knew. She'd never known him to be different, and I didn't want to burden her with my sadness at losing the father I'd known. But besides the worrying cough, Da wasn't really there, inside his head. He used to be full of life, but now... he slept all the time, yes. And when he wasn't sleeping, he was staring into the fire. Laney didn't remember the happy times, and I often thought he didn't even know who she was. He looked for me at least once a day, though, for the food and medicine I scrounged up, and at times there would be a spark of recognition in his eyes. But the spark would vanish as quickly as it came, and he'd go back to watching the fire from his pallet.

Despite what I'd told her, I didn't want Laney to have to deal with him. With any luck, I'd be halfway home before our father realized I was gone.

No such thing as luck, my inner voice said.

THE STARS SHONE like tiny pinpricks on a giant map in the sky—a good night for walking. I had seen few real maps, not since I was younger. That was before Laney was born, long before we had relocated to this godsforsaken place, scattered patches of land among a bog. The map had showed me places I hadn't even known existed, and I wondered if those places were any better than ours. Now, though, the stars were my guide, and I knew them as well as I knew the land.

The rest of the village was quiet, made up of dilapidated hovels on thin bridges of land divided by waterways and bogs. The stench of sickness and death occasionally wafted toward me, a smell I associated with this southern end of the vast, empty lands I called home. The Fell Marshes.

We'd had too many deaths lately, I thought as I ducked around the back of the house to meet Flint. And the land knew. It took our dead and sent them back to us as a stench on the wind. Or so the villagers thought, anyway.

A few villagers had crept off during winter. Some we never found, but the rest had died in the bog, their bodies ravaged by wild animals or monsters that migrated from The Desolation in the far south. Whether those lost villagers had died before or after their bones had been crunched between jaws, we never knew.

"What took so long?" Flint whispered when he saw me.

"Laney. Let's go."

Flint nodded, his mop of uncut red hair falling into his face. He brushed it aside and followed me. I set off through the garden that would grow nothing, trudging through shriveled-up stalks and dead soil. With the stars as our map, we left the beaten path, climbing over small land bridges, careful to avoid disturbing the water or the sleeping villagers, heading toward the deeper, wider waterway that flowed around our village. It was swift and treacherous, but if you knew where to step, there was a perfect ford leading across.

We picked our way cautiously over the stones, knowing the path by heart but unwilling to take a chance of getting dunked in the river. The frigid water seeped through my boots until pain shot through my ankles, but then we were across and hurrying into the forest.

We had a long climb ahead of us, out of the boggy lowlands and into the rocky foothills to the northeast. Uphill all the way.

The trees were quiet. No animals—explaining why hunters always came back empty-handed, and I was sick of eel for supper—not even the sound of a nightingale.

Flint hobbled beside me. The effort of keeping up was going to tax him much faster than it did me. Not that I was any healthier. The winter had been hard on us all. Like me, his shoulders were bony, and I knew that without his shirt, he looked skeletal. His cheekbones were sharp against his face, and though I hadn't looked in a mirror lately to confirm, mine were the same.

We needed food or a way to buy it. The villagers sometimes dried peat from the bog and sold it as fuel, and in other regions it might have been a lucrative undertaking, but most people in this area had some reason to stay hidden.

Like my family. We were far from most other settlements, and that's the way it had to be. I could pass for human most of the time, but Laney, like my deceased brother, could not. The fewer people who saw her for what she was, the better, which meant that even if we could afford a pony and cart, we couldn't take peat to the markets to the west or east, not with Laney. And it was too far a journey to leave my sister and father alone to fend for themselves for months at a time, so I couldn't go, either.

We were always hungry, catching eels and foraging for edible plants. On a rare morning, I shot something with my old bow, some animal that the predators hadn't already got to. I wished more than anything I could change circumstances for Laney, but an empty belly was better than having a sword stuck in it. So we got by the best we could.

"You know what Thomas did the other day?" Flint asked in a low voice.

I smiled, always enjoying the stories of his young son.

"Grabbed hold of the bed and said Dada, just looking right at me. He hasn't called Rose Mama yet."

It was too dark to see much, but I heard the pride in Flint's voice. He stopped, making me look around in alarm. "Everything's fine," he reassured me. His green eyes, normally merry, were brimming with some emotion I couldn't name. "I didn't understand before, you know. Not really."

"Understand what?" I frowned at this un-Flint-like behavior.

"Why you always protect Laney so fiercely, as though she's your own kid. Thomas…" Flint looked away and resumed walking, as though he couldn't face me while sharing his feelings. "He makes me want to be a better man, but not only that, he makes me want to make the whole world better, you know? For him. So he'll never have to go through what I did." He glanced over at me almost shyly.

I wanted to say something flippant but couldn't even speak around the lump in my throat, so I just nodded. *I know exactly, my friend. Exactly... even if the dream's impossible.*

He entertained me with more stories until we entered the darker part of the forest, where we could barely glimpse the stars through the twisted, gnarled branches above us. From there, we walked without speaking, the way as familiar to our feet as it was to our heads, so there was no need to talk. We couldn't risk alerting anyone—or anything—to our presence.

Upon entering the rocky foothills of the mountains to the north—treacherous not only for the terrain but because of what lurked among the shadows—a stone clattered ahead of us. In the absence of other noises, the isolated sound was eerily loud.

I froze, holding out a hand for Flint to stop. I didn't hear anything but his labored breathing, but I'd had too many close calls with predators that knew how to wait and hide just as well as I did.

Flint wore a deep frown. He didn't feel safe about proceeding, either, so we backtracked, retracing ground we'd already covered.

Over several hours, we trekked with hardly any rest, only pausing once so that Flint could regain his strength. When we had first started these missions, we had been stronger, hardier, and even Flint, with his inborn limp, hadn't needed as many rests. But now, at the end of a hard winter and without any goods to trade, nor any honest neighbors to trade with, we were weak. Our strength had leaked out of us like water seeping out of a wicker basket, and as the night wore on, we slowed. The only thing that kept us going was knowing we neared our destination.

Finally, we left the forest and entered the rockier country to the north, where the ravages of war were ever present. Our own little village was tucked away and had yet to be found, which was the only reason we had survived so long. But the rest of this land had not been spared. We avoided burned-out villages. They weren't empty; animals still lived there, human and otherwise. There was a ruined castle in the distance, one of its towers fallen, its stone blackened from a great fire. We avoided it, too.

We passed through the evidence of war and began to climb. We were nearly there, coming up the backside of what would turn into a deep ravine. At the bottom of the ravine was a road. It wasn't large or well-traveled, but a narrow twisty path that wound east to west.

We had learned a few things about this road over the years, most importantly that it was the only one still open in this region. Monsters and thieves plagued it, but if a merchant or army wanted to cross from Harrowfell and over the Fell Marshes, this was the road to use.

Flint and I called it The Throat, a place where bluffs rose over both sides of the road, which narrowed to pass through the gap. It was a perfect place for a couple of thieves to lie in wait, and an ideal place for an ambush.

Flint was more comfortable climbing than walking. His bowed right leg wasn't good for getting purchase on the rocks, but he moved just fine with the strength of his arms, shoulders, and other leg, faster than I did.

At the top, I paused to catch my breath, looking at how the position of the stars had changed. Then I eased down onto my belly and crawled toward the edge. Flint followed me.

There was no one on the road yet. The merchant wagons never traveled at night, and they wouldn't pass this way until at least after dawn. But we were here and prepared.

"I wish I could just sprout wings and jump down on them from here," Flint said. "If only I could fly."

"Then you should have been the son of an eagle instead of a peasant," I said with a smile.

He nudged my shoulder with his own. "I'd be a half-breed then, like you."

If anyone else had used that word, I would have slapped them, but Flint was the one person in the world who didn't judge me for what I was. Even my father...

I went quiet, thinking of Laney and how I wished things could be different for her. "You don't want that."

Flint flung his arm around my shoulders. "If you weren't a half-breed, Rose and Thomas would have starved long ago. I might have, too, because no one will hire a cripple."

I squeezed the hand on my shoulder. "You know I don't like it when you call yourself that. You are so much more than that."

"Just as you are so much more than your half-breed status. Anyway," Flint said, removing his arm and changing the subject, "I wonder what it would've been like to have been born with money, or to be one of these merchants who trade with different kingdoms."

It was a conversation we'd had many times over the years, since Flint's parents had died when he was a kid and he'd come to live with our family. "You wouldn't be spending your early morning hours lying in the dirt," I said, "but maybe you wouldn't have met Rose."

"True. And I wouldn't have met you, my friend."

Suddenly, there was a lump in my throat that I couldn't seem to clear. I wasn't prone to crying about much, so it was a testament to how hard these last few months had been. Flint's affection meant a lot to me. He was someone my age to talk to, a soul who understood me. We had been instant friends when we'd met, and that friendship had never changed. Now more than ever, I leaned on him. My father had long ago stopped communicating much beyond asking for food, and if I didn't have Flint...

I stopped that line of thinking. There was no point in going down that road.

"If I was rich, I would have better shoes," I said. The soles of my feet ached at this point, and they were still cold even though we had left the water far behind. I would have lined them with rabbit fur if there had been any rabbits to catch. But even rabbits didn't like living in the bog.

"We'll get you better shoes. I better get into position," Flint said. "We follow the plan, yeah?"

"Yes," I said with a sigh. "Always."

"Always," he repeated, lowering his body over the edge of the ravine. "See you on the other side."

He always said that, as if we were going to die and would see each other in whatever afterlife there was to meet us, if there was one at all.

I resisted the urge to roll my eyes and listened as he climbed down. He was a better climber than I, swifter with his hands, so he got to do the most dangerous work. Although my position wasn't exactly safe, Flint would be easier to catch if anyone spotted him. But he could climb out of the Throat more quickly than I could, if necessary.

The plan was always simple. I stopped the wagons, and Flint started stealing. Then we carried our loot home. The rule was we only took what we could carry.

I hoped to find some gold this time, and maybe some flour for bread. Seeds were useless to us because nothing would grow in the bog. But if we had coin, we could buy what we needed.

Still, I wouldn't mind trying to grow a garden this summer. Maybe I just hadn't planted the right things. I hadn't tried onions, for instance. I grimaced, thinking how unappealing it would be to survive on just onions and nothing else.

Better than starving and wondering if a person could live off just onions. I'd always wanted a vegetable garden beside a warm, comfortable house and a roof that didn't leak when it rained. My mother had taught me how to grow things, but that was before we had moved to a place where nothing would grow, and stealing was my best option.

The merchants, on the other hand, had grown fat off the wars of the last two decades. And while some of the smaller trading businesses had perished along the way, the merchants who succeeded had gold on every finger and every ear. I'd seen their horses and their clothes. Always the finest—stunning and well cared for.

I never felt bad about taking from them, not when the lives of my family members were at stake. And they always were. There was no work to be had here, only monsters. And I'd heard that in the cities it was worse, that women like me were forced into prostitution or even sold as slaves if they couldn't pay their debts. And since my father couldn't travel, and my sister needed to be in hiding, this was our only option. The land couldn't provide for us, so I had to use other means to survive.

I hadn't completely ruled out selling my body, knowing that my half-breed status, while usually repellent, would attract a certain clientele and their fetishes. Prostitution wasn't even an option, though, because it brought the same problems as any other job—I couldn't leave my family, and I couldn't take them with me.

For now, thieving would have to do.

The waiting felt monotonous, but really it was only an hour or so. As the first rays of light touched the road, I shifted to wake my sleeping limbs. Flint was out of sight, and now all we had to do was wait until the carts made an appearance.

But what came over the ravine was not just a single cart and a couple of armed men. There were three wagons and ten guards. Larger than any shipment we had intercepted thus far. The wagons were plain and driven by soldiers. Not merchants.

My heart hammered in my chest as I considered the consequences. A large shipment meant more possibility of gold and things that we could use, but I'd never dealt with this many guards. I would be stretching my talent to its limit.

For a moment, I hesitated, wavering in indecision as the carts bumped over the rocky ground.

Flint was waiting, and if I didn't intercept this party, we might not have another chance for several months. And that was simply too long. My father wouldn't survive, and Laney probably wouldn't, either. Neither would Thomas. It was this or leave our homes to brave the open, cruel world once again.

I simply refused to do that.

So I remained still, listening to the sound of the horses' hooves on the road and the clattering of the carts behind them. From my vantage point, I saw that the guards were well-armed, with leather armor and long swords. The wagons were large and without markings, and I wondered what they contained.

Finally, the wagons reached the tree where Flint was hiding. I waited until the final guard passed him, took a deep breath, and began to sing.

CHAPTER TWO

It was an old song, one my Nan sang to me when I was very small. A folk song that spoke of happier times, a nursery song. But I always added a twist to it, changed it from a song about a child riding a happy pony to one fleeing a rabid wolf. Old tune, new verse. My verse. Happiness always seemed just out of reach, and a song about a wolf rampaging through the village seemed fitting.

Below, the procession stopped, the horses tossing their heads and then going still, as if asleep. For a moment, the men riding or driving them raised their voices in anger. But then that too faded away.

I kept up the song for several minutes to make sure everyone was asleep, even those at the back of the line. Heads bowed low, resting on their chests, and the horses relaxed where they stood. Intention was key, and I avoided thinking about Flint so he wouldn't fall under the spell of my song.

Depending on the number of the company, it could

take several minutes to fully subdue them, but finally all of them were still. One of the soldiers had dismounted, lain down in the middle of the road, and begun to snore.

I stopped singing, then stood and waved at Flint, who emerged from the trees and hobbled as quickly as possible to the last cart in the line. Quickly, he threw off the canvas covering the goods and began to look for anything light enough to carry away.

It took me longer than I liked to get down from my vantage point, and by the time I reached the road, Flint was checking the final wagon. It was at the very front of the line, and I hurried toward him to relieve him of items he'd been carrying.

He found several sacks of flour, some fine leather that would make great boots, a bag of grain, and a bag of seeds —because I never stopped hoping for a garden. I stuffed all these into my satchel, except for the sack of flour, which I'd have to carry.

Flint was banging around the front of the wagon with his fist. We had done this many times and knew all the tricks, and soon, a false door fell open.

"I'll be damned," he breathed.

I peered over his shoulder. Inside a narrow cavity that ran underneath the driver's bench was a small chest. It was locked, but when Flint shook it, there was the distinct rattle of coins. And it was heavy.

The driver was slumped over, the reins slack in his hands, his cheek mashed against the seat. Quick as a wink, Flint climbed into the front of the wagon and searched his pockets. Then my friend turned and looked down at me with a grin.

There was a key in his hand. He handed it to me, and I inserted it quickly into the lock.

When the chest opened, I stood and gaped, stunned. The gold was as bright and shiny as any I had ever seen. It would feed my family—and the village—for the rest of the year, maybe longer. Quickly, I dumped the contents of my satchel and replaced them with the chest.

"Look," Flint said. He had climbed down and was reaching into the wagon once again.

Behind the chest of coins there was another small sack, at the far back of the hidey hole. It was just out of Flint's reach, and he had jammed his shoulder up against the wagon to get it.

I tapped him on the shoulder. "Let me try. The spell will wear off soon," I said, glancing at one of the guards, who still snoozed on his horse. But the horse flicked an ear, reminding me that my time was short. I changed places with my friend, reaching as far into the cavity as I could, but it was just out of reach. Looking around, I searched for something to use as a hook. My knife was too short.

"Leave it and let's get out of here with what we can," Flint said. "We got more than we bargained for already."

"I think I can reach it," I said, standing on a wagon wheel and peering into the wagon.

A horse stamped its hoof.

"Samara," Flint warned. "Let's go."

Sighing, I whispered, "But what would be more important than the gold? Isn't that why they hid it *behind* the coin? Because it was valuable?"

He had been looking over his shoulder, and he glanced back. I could tell he was thinking about it.

A horse snorted, and Flint shook his head. "No time," he hissed, grabbing my sleeve.

I allowed him to pull me down the road, where the ravine opened into a hill of large boulders interspersed with trees. Flint was right, of course. I'd have to forget the mysterious package. Now, secrecy was our best bet, and before we could go home, we had to create a false trail into the woods. It would take us the long way around, but we couldn't risk leading anyone to the village. And we didn't have a moment to spare.

The heavy chest of gold was slowing me down, the strap cutting into my shoulder. Flint climbed ahead, his steps swift and sure. He held out his hand for the satchel, and I handed it to him while I climbed up. I picked my way over rocks again, leading the way and purposely leaving a few footprints and scuff marks to follow.

Behind me, I heard Flint struggle to climb a boulder, so I turned to ask for the satchel again.

But when I looked behind, my words froze in my throat.

There was a soldier on horseback, just at the bottom of the rocks. He was sitting astride his horse, looking straight at me.

I froze. There was nowhere to hide. The shadows of the trees overhead weren't enough to conceal us. But the soldier wasn't giving chase, and I wondered why. Maybe he was still dazed from my earlier song. If so, maybe we still had a chance to get away.

Around us, armed men materialized out of the shadows, like they had been there all along and had been concealed by some magic. My entire body grew cold when I realized we were surrounded.

Flint hadn't seen them yet and was still pulling himself up a rock.

"Flint!" I yelled in warning. Too late.

He looked up at me and then cried out. His face twisted in agony, and he fell forward with an arrow sticking out of his back.

No. I tried to begin singing, to stop the soldiers from doing anything else, but my throat was closing up in fear.

With a strangled cry, I began to climb down to my friend. He was still alive, struggling to stand but not finding his feet. I reached him just as another arrow sank into his back. I tried to catch his arm but missed. Without even a cry, Flint fell. This time, he went to the side, tumbling down the rocks.

The satchel fell with Flint, the box breaking open and spilling coins into the nooks and crannies. But I didn't care. All I could do was watch helplessly as he collapsed.

Another arrow struck the rocks just beside my thigh, and I jumped away, slipping and falling down on the other side of the boulder and losing sight of Flint.

I hit my head and the world spun, but despite the blood flowing down my face, I spied a dense patch of brush. Beneath it was a narrow space, and I began to crawl for it, hoping to lose the larger soldiers.

"Flint!" I yelled. The time for secrecy was long gone, and I hoped beyond hope that my friend would answer. Instead, I heard the shouts of the soldiers on my trail, clambering over the rocks and calling to one another.

Just as I reached the brush, a searing pain shot through my calf. An arrow had sliced through the outer layer of skin, but not stuck. It hurt like hell but wouldn't slow me down.

Ignoring the fire in my leg and the pounding in my head, I slid under the coarse brush, which scratched my cheeks and hands and opened tiny new wounds. The slope went upward, and I scrambled to crawl through the brush-covered rocks and stay under cover. My bow, slung over my shoulder, got caught on a branch. Unable to move backward or forward, I almost panicked. But instead, I took my knife and cut the straps on my bow and quiver of arrows. I left them behind as I crawled on my belly, away from the soldiers.

Cursing, the guards began climbing up after me, hacking through the brush with axes or swords, wolves hunting a rabbit. I had the advantage of being small enough to hide, but I was outnumbered, and for all I knew, surrounded.

And then came the sound I had been dreading. The distinct slicing of a sword going through flesh.

They had killed Flint. I didn't have to see to know. I had heard such a sound before.

An invisible hand seemed to squeeze my heart, and I almost collapsed. But I pushed the sounds away and slipped into a shallow depression. Out from the cover of the brush, I was an easy target, so I jumped to my feet to make a dash for the forest.

At any moment, I expected to feel the pain of an

arrow in my spine or ribs, and I hoped I died quickly. I wasn't afraid of pain, but I didn't want to be a plaything for the soldiers. But though I heard lots of shouting, nothing hit me, and a cold chill ran down my spine despite the sweat.

They wanted me alive.

A number of horrors sprang to mind as I thought about why, but I pushed them aside in favor of running. I'd rather die fighting than let them catch me, but there was no shame in running.

Pushing through a particularly dense outcrop of thorny bushes, I came out in the open to a steep drop, an almost vertical plunge of twenty feet. I couldn't jump without worrying about twisting an ankle, but unless I wanted to sit and wait for them to catch me, I had to press forward.

I swung my body over the edge, kicking my feet around to look for purchase. Finally, I found a tentative foothold and lowered my weight onto it. Then I found another and used it, praying to whatever gods existed to not let my sweaty hands slip.

The guards' heavy footsteps grew closer. At any moment I'd be staring down the wrong end of a crossbow.

I'd run out of time. Without looking up, I risked the fall and jumped the rest of the way, intentionally crumpling my body to absorb the shock of the impact.

The jump could have been worse, but it still dazed me. Getting to my feet, I bolted for the woods without looking back. There was no point now, and it would only slow me down, so I ran flat out for the cover of the trees.

But I was on open ground, and horses' hooves

approached from my right. Mounted riders would have no problem catching me. Sensing one of them come up from behind, I threw myself to the ground and rolled under the first of the trees. A crossbow bolt slammed into the tree next to me. It had been shot low, to hit my leg, maybe, confirming my suspicion that they didn't want to kill me, just slow me down long enough to catch me.

Scrambling to my feet, I darted into the dark forest, hoping to get lost quickly. But these riders didn't fear the forest as I'd hoped, and I heard them plunge in.

I risked a glance back, surprised when I didn't see anyone. But I could still hear horses' hooves and the occasional shout. Backing behind a large tree, I prayed the soldiers hadn't brought hounds with them. If so, there was a chance I could get away.

But without Flint.

I brushed the blood out of my eyes with the back of my dirty hand. Even in late morning, this part of the forest stayed dark, with the ancient, thickly growing trees and vines blocking out the sun. That was to my advantage.

A twig snapped close by, too close for comfort. Peering around, I made a dash for another cluster and pulled myself into the crook of a dense overhanging tree that was covered in shadow. The smell of earth and forest decay was strong here, too sharp to be pleasant. But I ignored it and paused to listen.

There were no other noises, and even the sounds of soldiers and their horses had faded. The hairs on the back of my neck prickled, though, like I was being watched.

Or hunted by something other than the soldiers.

By deadly creatures no monster hunter had ever been able to catch. It was very possible, in these woods. I remembered the rocks Flint and I had avoided on our way to The Throat, and the feeling of being watched then, as well. I looked up, down, and all around, peering into every shadow and sunbeam. I could try to sing and enchant whatever it was, but then I would give myself away to the soldiers, who were too far away and too spread out to be affected by it. And my songs didn't always work on creatures. People, yes, but not monsters.

But the thought of being torn limb from limb or eaten alive didn't appeal to me either, and I had to make a decision. Find another hiding spot and risk attracting the soldiers, or remain in place and fight off whatever was lurking nearby. I wasn't much to look at as far as meat on my bones. But to a creature that was equally starving, I might have been a three-course meal. Better to stay hidden, and wait.

Then I thought about Laney, about Flint's wife and baby boy. I had to get home; I couldn't bear for Rose not to know what had happened. I had learned at a young age that disappearance was worse than death. At least death was final and there was no wondering.

Death, we had learned to deal with.

And if I never returned, my family had little chance of surviving. Laney was too young to take care of my father, and she had to stay hidden. Rose would help them, though. She would look out for them until I could get back.

The thought gave me courage, and I felt a surge of

strength. I had to do *something*. If I stayed here, something or someone would find me. It was time to move.

Before I got out of my hiding place, though, there was a horrifying shriek, followed by the sound of cracking limbs and branches.

There were more shouts, and soldiers cursing and yelling. Then another cry of anguish followed by a roar.

There *had* been a monster lurking nearby, and it sounded like it had nabbed a well-fed soldier for its meal instead of me.

Breathing a sigh of relief, and not feeling at all sorry, I lowered myself to the ground and crept through the trees.

My brown clothes and hood blended into the shadows. The blood and dirt striping my face would also add concealment. Hiding should have been easy, and yet the farther I went, the more I knew I was being watched. I hadn't heard the soldiers for some time, and that troubled me. Unless there was a pack of monsters to eat them, they had gone quiet for another reason. I hadn't gone far enough to lose them, which meant that something else had waylaid them, or they had stopped looking. And there was no reason for them to have stopped looking.

Unless they knew I couldn't get away.

The thought hit me as suddenly as if I had jumped into an icy stream. Fear flowed over my body, heightening my senses and threatening to freeze me where I stood.

On instinct, I listened. I should have heard some birds or insects. Something. Whatever was causing the silence was not revealing itself. And that was bad, very bad. It implied intelligence, or evil. Both, maybe. Something that preferred to stalk its prey and terrify it before it died. I'd heard of monsters that loved the taste of fear in their prey's blood, from the rush that came with a body under stress. But I kept my wits about me and didn't panic, instead opening all my senses to the forest around me.

There was an earthy smell, one that I expected, but overlaid with a hint of something bitter and strong. The occasional breeze rustled the branches above but didn't make its way to the ground. The faint movement of air brushed my lips, but no more than that. The earth beneath my feet was solid and comforting. Giant black trunks rose hundreds of feet into the air, but the atmosphere was clear.

The shadows changed as I waited, but none of them contained the monster that was hunting me. It had to be another monster, and I had left my hiding spot behind. Finally, what caught my attention wasn't the movement of shadows, but a beam of light. It glinted off something moving toward me.

I couldn't tell what it was but I calmed my breathing, kept my position, and watched. The movement was subtle and reminded me of the way a breeze ripples over water. Something was moving the air. It could have been some sort of shadow monster that could conceal itself within the background of the forest. But I didn't think so —it was something else, something less material and more terrifying.

As the air moved closer to me, I decided I didn't have any choice.

I opened my mouth and took a deep breath, ready to sing and paralyze whatever crept toward me.

But when I did, once again, no sound came out. This time, it was as if an invisible hand was clutching my throat instead of my heart. I clawed at my throat and tried to scream, but all that came out was a hollow rasping noise.

Terrified, I watched that movement come toward me and turned to run, but the air was shimmering all around me now. As my heart tried to live in my throat, I thought that perhaps it was fitting that I died this way, and that after what happened to Flint, I didn't deserve to live. But I drew my knife anyway, prepared to fight until the death.

"There is no need for that, girl," came a voice from right behind me.

I swung around, keeping my knife in front of me, and was surprised by a gasp of pain. Then there was a flash of pain in my knuckles, and the knife was knocked out of my hand.

I was like a wild animal caught in a trap, wheeling my arms to lash out at anything else that might be close. But I felt nothing.

Instead of waiting for the trap to close, I tried to bolt away from the moving air and the voice.

But I only made it a few steps when I ran into something solid. Something that hadn't been there a second ago.

I fell to the ground, jarred as if I'd rammed into solid stone.

My head swam, and a figure appeared, standing over me dressed in a black cloak with a hood. They wore a silver mask that covered their entire face, with two holes for the eyes. I couldn't tell if they were a man or a woman, but it didn't much matter. The embroidery around the hood and on the edge the cloak, not to mention the mask, told me who they were.

A Deviant. A mage that served The Harrow.

He had many names, but I'd only ever heard "The Harrow." A self-appointed king who was never satisfied with what he'd already taken. He always wanted more. A conqueror, butcher, and oppressor.

And he hated half-breeds. Anything that wasn't human, really, but half-breeds especially.

He was the reason I lived in fear. The reason I had lost my brother all those years ago. The reason Laney couldn't show her face in public.

The presence of a Deviant and soldiers so close to my home set my bones to shaking. It was my worst nightmare because it only meant one thing.

They were hunting.

I shuddered. I had no love for the mages, many of whom were just sadistic witch-hunters. And I had seen what the Deviants did to anyone in their way, or even just for sport. The soldiers had brought a mage with them, and that's why I hadn't been able to sing. It's why they had been able to hide in ambush, waiting for Flint and me.

I scrambled backward, thinking that the Deviant would set me on fire and watch me burn.

But the Deviant didn't move. Instead, he spoke again. And yes, this time I recognized a man's voice. "We've been looking for you for some time, thief. Running is futile, as you have guessed. But the triumph is worth the chase, I always say."

Out of the corner of my eye, I saw my knife, and reached for it.

Someone kicked my hand, and I gasped with pain. Looking up, I saw two soldiers standing over me as well, their short swords pointed my way. One of them had kicked my hand with his pointed steel boots, and my bones were already throbbing with pain. There was fresh blood on my knuckles.

Now that they were close, I saw a strange crest on their armor—a red serpent on a gold background.

"Take her," was all the mage said. And then there were strong, rough hands on my arms, and a forced march through the forest.

CHAPTER THREE

They had beheaded Flint.

From where I was tied, I could see his bright red hair splayed across a boulder like a gruesome flower. I wanted to scream, to rage at the injustice of it all.

I'd heard stories, knew what was coming. And when the first soldier began leering at me as I lay there with my wrists bound behind my back and my ankles tied to a tree, I knew what he had on his mind. I'd seen that look before. There was a hunger there, a dirty hunger, like a starving man who resorts to cannibalism to satisfy that ache in his belly.

I wanted to hurl obscenities at him but couldn't. My throat was dry, mouth parched from lack of water and from whatever spell the mage had used on me. Instead, I got to my knees and glared daggers at the man.

"We've got a wild one," he said. The soldier laughed and grabbed his balls, and the other soldiers looked on in interest. And when the first man unbuckled his belt, I vowed to take a chunk of his flesh, even if I had to tear it from him with my own teeth. I knew it wouldn't stop what was coming, but I would take my revenge.

But as the man marched over to me, undoing his trousers and preparing to show me whatever small thing resided inside them, the Deviant spoke.

"She is of siren blood, didn't you hear me?"

The soldier paused, his eyes on my breasts and legs, his hand still in his pants.

"If you take her," the mage said, "it will be like fucking a monster. And the gods see that as an abomination." He raised his voice. "Any man who takes her will be cursed. She is worse than a witch. Worse than a horse. Worse than a sheep."

Heat burned my cheeks. It wasn't the first time I had heard such talk, but it was the first time I was grateful for it. The soldier paused his advance and glanced at the mage. Then he looked back at me, and I could see the lust in his eyes warring with disgust.

The Deviant was correct about one thing, though I didn't know how. I was of siren blood. My great-grandmother had been a full siren, and that made me an outcast. I didn't have any outward signs, only the gift of my song. In that regard, I was fortunate. My sister, like my brother, looked different. They didn't look completely human. I did, though, and if the Deviant hadn't said something, however insulting, things might have gone differently.

Finally, the soldier's disgust won out. He let go of his balls, buckled his belt, and, as if to punish me for tempting me, kicked me hard in the belly.

I doubled over in pain, the breath pushing out of me like a bellows. Coughing, I tried to speak, but the mage's spell still had a hold on me. Instead, I satisfied myself with glaring at first the soldier and then the mage, making eye contact through his mask.

The soldier kicked me again, this time catching my jaw with his toe, and I fell. Dirt invaded my lungs as I tried to breathe through the pain, and I coughed and sputtered.

The mage held up a staying hand, and before leaving me alone, the soldier spat on my face. The spittle trailed down my bloodied cheek into my open mouth, and I gagged.

"There is a bounty on your head, did you know?" the mage asked, as if I wasn't currently fighting for every breath. His crooked staff rested on the tree behind him. "When I heard about the strange occurrences in these mountains, about a witch who holds an entire caravan of men under her spell while she robs them blind, I was intrigued. There were merchants who swore that their deliveries would have been on time, or that they hadn't been short of supplies when they left, and I knew there was something worth investigating. Those men were whipped or beaten to within an inch of their lives for stealing, but they hadn't committed the crime. And neither had a witch. You are a siren." He said the word as if spitting it. "An evil woman who is more monster than anything else. How dare you walk among us as if you were human? How dare you use your wiles to stop honest, hardworking folk?"

There was a venom in the Deviant's voice that sent a

shiver down my spine, and I forgot about the pain in my stomach and jaw. It was replaced with anger.

All I wanted was to survive and live in peace. Instead, I was hunted for being different. And now my friend was dead, his life snuffed out as if it meant nothing.

But it had meant something to me, and to Rose and Thomas.

"I monitored these rumors," he continued. "I knew what I was seeking, and so I prepared myself and brought the soldiers here to find you."

I was glaring at the mage now as if I could kill him with my eyes, but it only made him laugh. "You know," he said as if he were talking to a friend, "I could sell you to one of those traveling shows, as a freak of nature. And they would let men pay to see you in a cage, or allow them to use you to satisfy their unholy lusts. It is a good thing, siren, that I have found you instead of anyone else. In keeping you for myself, I will be saving men from themselves, those who are weak and cannot withstand your lustful advances, or the spell of your beguiling voice.

"Some people would burn you alive. It is only what you deserve, and what The Harrow's law demands. Perhaps..." The Deviant raised his head and I saw a flash in his eyes. Eyes that were still hidden behind his cowardly mask. "And yet, perhaps you *desire* to be sold. Perhaps you would like to be known for what you are—a half-breed and a thief. Tell me, who tipped you off about the wagons?"

The question was abrupt, and even if I wanted to, I

couldn't answer him. My voice wouldn't work. The Deviant obviously knew this because I felt his laughter even though I couldn't see it on his face.

"Don't want to talk? I have ways, you know, siren. Ways of making you wish you'd never been born out of your filthy mother's womb."

I struggled on the ground, wrenching at my bonds and grimacing as they cut into my wrists.

"You will tell me who your spy is, or you will pay. And then after that, I'll make sure your family pays, too. You have a family, yes? Was that cripple over there your husband? Do you have filthy children? Don't even try to lie. I see the fear on your face." And then he stood and began walking toward me, lifting his robes off the ground as if he were afraid I'd get them dirty. He leaned over me and lowered his voice. "I will find your children and I will kill them in front of you. Slowly, and with much pain. You know I will. It'll be easier if you just cooperate. Or... perhaps I will kill you and sell *them* to the freak shows. So many enticing options."

Don't show him your fear. Don't give him leverage.

The mages didn't claim to be human, but to be supernatural beings that walked the earth by the grace of their magic. This man, this creature, had a lust in him which had nothing to do with sex. He thrived on pain and suffering, and reeked of ill-gotten power. But to me, he seemed completely human. And evil. It didn't take magic to make a monster.

At last, the effects of the spell begin to wear off, and I croaked out a harsh "no."

The Deviant cackled and produced a long, cruel-looking silver dagger from his robes.

But instead of waiting for him to use it, I jerked forward, tensing my bruised stomach muscles, and sank my teeth into his exposed ankle.

And then three things happened very quickly.

There was a sharp pain in my ear as the mage struck me; the soldiers shouted and drew their swords; and an almost inhuman cry of rage descended upon the camp.

Something warm and wet splashed my face, and then the mage's flesh was torn out from between my teeth. I tasted his blood and spat it out, and then looked just in time to see him fall heavily to the ground. His head rolled separately from his body, rolling away as if it were child's hideous ball, the mask still in place.

There was a new man, dressed from head to toe in black and wearing a black cloak, fighting all the soldiers at once. He bore a long sword that seemed to catch the light like a shining beacon, with runes that glowed, and he began slicing the soldiers into bits.

I had rarely seen any real sword fighting. Most of my experience had been on the receiving end, with soldiers punishing unarmed common folk. But even with my limited understanding, I quickly realized that this man knew what he was doing. He lunged, stabbing a man through the heart before pulling his sword out and chopping another man's head off in the same motion. He turned and sliced another man's arm at the elbow. The man went down screaming, but his cry was cut short as the man in black pressed the glowing blade into his throat. And then, the world was a blur of steel and cries and blood.

The man in black almost danced with his sword, as if it were part of him, and for all I knew it had sprung from his hands using magic. He cut his way through the entire camp, not letting one soldier go free, and not seeming to take any blows of his own. He far outmatched any of them in skill, and by the time he was done, his body splattered with the blood of his enemies, my mouth was gaping open. He stood among the ring of bodies, whirling around with his sword as if checking to make sure no one had gotten away.

For a moment I was in awe of him, and then I remembered my own predicament. He had a sword, and I was tied up. And just because he had killed my captors didn't mean he had good intentions for me. Belatedly, I struggled to sit up, looking around for any dropped swords or knives within reach.

And then the stranger stomped over to me and turned me over with his foot. There was an ugly look in his eyes, one that was different from the outward lust of the mage and soldiers, and yet even more dangerous.

My voice was still recovering, but I was able to croak something out. "Just kill me," I rasped.

Instead, the man didn't speak but grabbed my arm and pulled me roughly to a sitting position against the tree. I struggled, but there wasn't much I could do. My mouth still tasted of the Deviant's blood, and my jaw was on fire, but I supposed I could use my teeth on this man, as well, if I had to. However, he was careful to keep out of reach, as if he had seen what I'd done to the mage.

"Stay there," he commanded. Then he turned, and without another glance at me, began rifling through the mage's pockets. While he searched, I had a moment to study him.

The stranger's face was a bit angular, with a sharp jaw, nose, and cheekbones, as if he had faced his own struggles with starvation. But his body was fit as any I'd ever seen. It was lean; his muscles bulged from beneath his leather armor and the fine fabric covering his thighs.

Finally, the man in black turned to glare at me. His dark hair fell to his shoulders, halfway covering his face and piercing, hazel eyes.

"If you won't kill me, then let me go," I whispered. It was as much as I could manage; my throat was hoarse and raw. The mage's spell had done damage, it seemed. As if I'd spent the entire day singing, or had come down with a bad illness.

The warrior ignored me and continued searching all the soldiers' bodies. He basically stripped them, and each time he finished, he seemingly came up with nothing. His dark look turned even darker, and he returned to search the mage again. This time, he practically tore the Deviant's robes in his effort.

"What are you looking for?" I asked.

Finally, the man in black turned to me, and I didn't like the look in his eye one bit. It spoke of death. Still, I preferred it to leering looks from the soldiers.

"Where is it?" he asked. He came over to me again and began patting me down, turning out my pockets.

I struggled. "Get your hands off me!"

But he didn't pay attention, running his hands down

my legs and even pulling off my worn leather boots to check inside them. The cold air made my toes curl. "What are you looking for?" I asked again. "Stop touching me. Or are you like that mage over there?"

The man in black stopped his searching and sat back, crouching next to me. "I am nothing like him," he said in a low voice.

"And yet you take your liberties with me just as he would have done. You are no better."

The stranger grabbed my shoulders and shook me. "Where is it?" he asked, enunciating every word. "I know you took it."

"I don't know what you're talking about. Unless you mean the gold?" I nodded toward where I could still see Flint's poor body lying among the boulders. "If you..." I bit back a sob and then glared at him. "It's there."

But he only scowled. "Not the fucking gold. You know what I want. Where did you hide it? In the forest?" He had a strange accent, one I couldn't place.

And then he grabbed my shoulders once again and hauled me to my feet.

I wobbled slightly but shook my head. "I don't know what you're talking about."

My voice was still raw and every word was agony, but my strength was returning. Whatever he was searching for, I wasn't about to help him. It was obvious that he hadn't saved me for my sake, only for his own ends. And I wasn't going to reward that, even if I could.

"Why did they bring a mage just for you?" he asked, holding me firmly.

I wondered the same thing myself, but I couldn't say.

I had never taken enough money to draw much attention. Flint and I were thieves, but we knew that if we ever stole too much, they would hunt us to the ends of the earth.

"I'll ask you again," the man said dangerously. "That package that was on the wagon. Where is it?"

I glared at him, putting as much venom into it as I could. After everything that had happened today, after Flint... I just didn't have the patience for ridiculous questions. The mage had seemed to think I had an informant. I didn't. I just knew the route and listened for the right information. "I don't know what you're talking about. Now let me go."

This last sentence was stronger than anything yet, and I knew that soon I'd be able to sing again.

The ability had always been with me, and there was a rush of feeling that always happened right before the magic began to work. If I could just stay alive long enough, I could put this man in a trance and get free.

And then I remembered something, and it put singing out of my mind for the moment. "That package on the wagon? We didn't take it."

With a swift, precise movements, he cut the bonds around my ankles with his dagger. Then he grabbed my arm again. "Where on the wagon? Show me."

And he began marching me down the road toward the wagons.

When we arrived, I stifled a gasp.

Corpses were everywhere, lying with throats slit and heads separated from bodies, soaking the ground with blood. All the drivers, along with the ten soldiers, were dead.

The horses startled at seeing us, but the man in black began speaking in low tones to calm them, and half-dragged me to the front wagon. The secret door that Flint and I had found was still open, but there was nothing inside.

I shook my head. "There was a sack in here, but we didn't take it. We were after the gold. If you don't believe me, go check my friend's body, that is, if the soldiers haven't taken everything from it. There was a chest of at least thirty gold coins scattered on the rocks."

The man in black narrowed his eyes and glared at me, shaking my arm again.

"Shaking me isn't going to do you any good," I spat. "And if you continue to do that, I'll take a chunk out of you just like I did the mage."

It was an empty threat, and we both knew it. The mage had taken me for granted, but this man looked smarter.

"Who killed these men?" I asked finally.

"I thought you did," my captor said.

I laughed. I couldn't help it, but the strain must have finally made me crack, because I began laughing and couldn't stop. Everything seemed too surreal, too ridiculous. And yet, before long, I realized I was only laughing because if I didn't, I would break down in grief.

My captor stared at me warily until I got myself under control.

"We just wanted the gold and some flour for bread," I whispered. I stared at the empty hiding place, wondering. If I hadn't hesitated so long, would Flint still be alive?

I knew the question would haunt me forever. If not

for the thought of my sister being all alone, and my father lying next to the fire, I would have asked the man in black to just kill me right there and then.

But I couldn't abandon my family, nor could I abandon Flint's, so I straightened and looked up at the dark-haired man standing next to me. "One of the soldiers must have taken it," I said. "It's the only thing that makes sense."

He shook his head, and briefly loosened his hold on my arm. "The original ten soldiers are all accounted for. If you don't have it and they don't have it, there was someone else who knew about it."

I raised an eyebrow. "Someone like you?"

He darted a glance at me but then began looking up at the surrounding hills. "Whoever it is, they'll be gone, but that doesn't mean they can't be found."

"Then let me go. I've got to make sure the soldiers haven't found my village."

For some reason, I thought that honesty would be the best option here. I didn't have any qualms about lying, but sometimes the truth meant more. The man looked at me for a moment, as if weighing something in his mind. Then he shook his head.

"So that you can go get the parcel and run away?" he asked.

"Fuck you," I said. "I don't have it, whatever it is. I told you. We were only after the gold and some flour."

"And there's no way in hell I'm going to trust you." The man began half dragging me back, and I resisted. He surprised me by lifting me easily and swinging me over his shoulder so that all I saw was the back of his flowing cloak.

I cursed him all the way back to the demolished camp. He set me down roughly against the same tree and tied me to it again. My arms, shoulders, jaw—really, my entire body—ached at this point. Blood was still trickling into my eye, and I had no way of brushing it away, now that my hands were tied behind me to the tree. "Please," I said, aware that I had never begged before, "let me go. More soldiers could be on their way right now."

"And if they are, you'll lead them straight back to your village. Or straight back to me."

"You bastard," I said. The pain—physical and emotional—was very real. The more I thought about it, the more I figured that the mage had sent soldiers to my village, that the entire thing had been set up from the very beginning. I had no idea what this man in black was about, but I didn't trust anything he said. I had to get away from him, had to make sure my family was okay. And that Flint's family would survive. It was the least I could do.

"Please," I said. But the man in black continued to ignore me and began searching the bodies anew, removing boots, cloaks, and armor that he hadn't searched before.

"Why didn't you kill me?" I whispered. More to myself than to him, but he must have heard me.

"Because I figured that if I didn't find what I was looking for here, that you would show me where it is."

I shook my head and sank back against the tree.

"You're right," I said softly. "If I tell you where it is, will you let me go?"

The man in black came over to me. "If you tell me where it is and I find it, I will let you go."

I looked up at him through my lashes, doing my best impersonation of a helpless woman. I had a lot of practice in my short twenty-two years. "At least untie my legs."

The swordsman shook his head.

I sighed heavily. "All right, I'll tell you," I said, injecting as much despondency into my voice as I could, hoping to incite pity. I didn't *expect* pity because I didn't expect a man like him to have any sort of empathy toward another person. But hopefully it would throw him off guard if he thought I had given up. He crouched next to me, and I looked up at him again.

And then I took a deep breath as if to sigh, and instead began to sing. This time, it was an old folk tune about the wolf who would run among the sheep and pick out the new lambs for its meal, preferring their tender meat to anything else in the world. A wolf that was smart and knew how to evade the hounds and the hunters who looked for it.

The man in black was stronger than I'd anticipated. He listened to my song, staring at me intently as if at first he was overwhelmed with it. But then he seemed to resist, steadying himself against the ground and glaring at me in anger. He had realized what was happening and obviously didn't like it. I wouldn't either, but my life literally depended on it.

He sat there, veins straining in his forehead and his

muscles seeming to clench as he tried to fight the song, but as my voice grew stronger, I sang louder, with everything in me.

The man in black sat back, still glaring at me and so obviously fighting it, but eventually he lay back and closed his eyes.

Not one to take anything for granted, I continued singing, eventually kicking him hard to make sure he was actually asleep. When I was certain he was knocked out, I strained against my bonds and scooted over to him. He had a dagger on his right hip, and I could just reach it. It didn't take much to shear my bonds away. It was probably the sharpest dagger I'd ever used.

It took a moment for feeling come back to my hands, and I was hurting everywhere, but the blood and chafing around my wrists only added to my fury. I thought about kicking him a few times, but getting away was more important.

Kill him. He'll only come after you when he wakes up, and he'll be even angrier.

But I had never killed anyone, and this stranger had saved me from the Deviant. In a way, I felt like I owed him. By leaving him alive, I figured we were even.

My own knife was nowhere to be seen, and they had taken my hood. Quickly, I removed my captor's belt, taking his dagger and putting it around my own waist. I also removed his sword and the belt that kept it tight across his back. The sword had a gold hilt that was covered in an intricate design. In the center was a bird in flight. I didn't look at them now, but I had seen the runes on the blade glow earlier when the man in black was fighting. I didn't know much about swords, but I knew enough to know this one was valuable. It only solidified my opinion of the arrogant, demanding man lying asleep at my feet. He *must* have been high born. He could afford another sword, and I could sell this one.

Throwing the strap over my shoulder, I removed two large golden rings from his fingers. One had the image of a raven, like his sword. The other was more delicately crafted, with what looked like branches set around a ruby. I then felt around his unconscious body and found a small bag of coins. Tucking the rings into the pouch, and the pouch into my new belt, I worked to remove his long cloak. The cloak and hood would be warm in the forest, and I threw them over everything, over my blood-stained clothes and new weapons.

And then, unable to resist a final kick to his ribs, I turned and ran.

The first thing I did was find Flint's body. Everything within me told me to run home, but I couldn't just leave him without saying goodbye. The man in black wouldn't stay unconscious long, and since I'd never had anyone able to resist me like he did, I didn't even fully trust that he would stay out any length of time.

Which meant I didn't have time to bury my friend. I climbed the boulders, gingerly picking up his head and placing it next to his body. Then, I laid my head on his chest and threw an arm over his bony body. Tears rolled down my cheeks.

"I love you, Flint."

He had been like a brother to me all these years, and

we'd always looked out for each other. And now the sense of loss at his passing was almost more than I could bear. But I had a purpose, and for now that would keep me going. The coins were gone, but the broken chest lay nearby. I picked it up and flung it away. Then, I said farewell one more time before taking off for home.

CHAPTER FOUR

I was hungry and thirsty, and I couldn't stop looking over my shoulder. There were enemies behind every tree, in every sound. But each time I looked, there was nothing.

As the sun was setting, I neared my home. On instinct, I went downriver, just in case someone was following me. Climbing down the muddy bank, I went straight for the water. The current flowed swiftly, having passed the islands that formed our village and with nothing to hinder it.

For the first time in hours, I drank. Then I splashed icy water on my face, neck, and injuries. Gingerly, I felt along my jawline. It still throbbed and was swollen, but it wasn't broken. My reflection in the water showed a painfully thin woman with haunted blue eyes, and I wasn't surprised by the dark circles that made my face look even more skeletal. My skin was pale despite spending most days outdoors, and the slight green undertone made me look sick, rather than give away my siren heritage. The scratches on my face had stopped bleeding, but my thick dark hair was tangled and had twigs sticking out of it. I looked like the wild woman the soldier had accused me of being. A bog witch. It might have been funny, something Flint and I could have laughed over...

With the surge of painful memories, I stopped looking at myself and splashed more cold water on my jaw to ease the pain.

Standing, I examined the path along the river, which wasn't a path at all but more like mud and silt flowing out of the bog. If I thought I could walk all the way upriver from here, I would have, and the bank would have mostly kept me hidden. The trek through the mud would be a struggle, though, and if anyone came upon my footprints, they would lead them straight to the village. The rapidly gathering dark was no guarantee my tracks would remain unseen.

With a sigh, I climbed the bank, placing each foot slowly as fatigue began to set in. I had just reached the top embankment when a leather-clad hand clasped over my mouth, and I was yanked bodily to the ground.

I hit the ground hard on my left side, adding to the pain already there. Panicking, I tried to scream, only to have the hand clamp down harder.

"Hush, you little witch," came the accented voice of the man in black. "Did you think I wouldn't find you? That I wouldn't catch you?"

I struggled more, elbowing him hard in the ribs. But his leather armor blunted some of the impact, and he didn't let go. So I reached back to scratch his eyes out.

My attacker jerked his head back, and then began

trying to pin me beneath his body, one leg wrapping around me while he tried to secure my flailing arms. He wasn't gentle, but that only made me fight harder. I was slippery when I wanted to be and moved every part of my body that was free.

I reached around, and without giving him a chance to catch me, found his balls and squeezed. He grunted and then jerked away but still didn't let go of my mouth. But I managed to open my jaws, and his finger slipped into my mouth. I clamped down on it, tasting blood through the leather.

The man yelled in pain and let go. Scrambling onto all fours, I reached for the dagger at my hip. But swift as thought, the man was on his feet with a sword at my throat. He must have picked one up from the dead soldiers because I still had his strapped across my back. Heaving, he was nursing his bleeding finger and panting hard. Good. I hoped I had bruised his balls.

Then, keeping his sword at my throat, he came in close and grabbed my wrist. Yanking me off my feet once more, he threw me to the ground. At this point the bruises were going to cover my entire body.

"Let me go," I said. But before I finished the words, he was pressing the tip of the blade under my chin.

"Don't speak until I tell you to." Then he held up his bleeding hand and looked at me. "Give me one reason why I shouldn't kill you right now."

"You mean I can speak, then?" I said with as much snark as I could muster. "Because you *just* said—"

He scowled and pressed the blade into my skin,

giving me just enough room to talk without cutting myself. "If you sing, I will slit your throat."

"I haven't done anything to you except try to get away," I said. "Can you blame me?"

"Tell me where it is," he demanded. "Dammit, woman, you don't know what you're playing at."

I lifted my chin just a hair. "You're right. I don't. And if you've been following me all day, then you know I don't have anything. Just blood and bruises to show for all my trouble."

"You expect me to believe you and that red-haired boy were working by yourselves?"

It was my turn to scowl. "That *boy* had a name, and he was more man than you'll ever be."

The insult didn't faze him. "Where are you from?"

I decided not to answer. He didn't deserve an answer, and even a lie could endanger my village, with it being so close. He'd just have to kill me.

"Answer me, witch. Where are your people?" he asked.

"I do not have people," I spat. "My friend and I were working alone, and the soldiers caught us and killed him. That's the truth. Haven't I endured enough for one day?"

But my play for sympathy didn't work. The man in black grabbed my arm and hauled me to my feet.

"I have no reason to believe you," he said, removing his belt from around my waist, his dagger along with it, and swapping the soldier's sword for his own. He checked the coin pouch and found the rings, which he put back on his fingers. "There was a mage after you, and mages aren't summoned for common thieves. But I'm not going to argue with you here in this monster-infested bog. Perhaps after a few days of hard walking, you'll change your mind."

And then he prodded me to move, his sword pressed into the nape of my neck.

I hissed and hurried forward, picking my way carefully in the near-total blackness, and we walked like that until the moon rose over the spongy ground. I listened to his every step, using every excuse to glance back at him. As soon as I got the chance, I'd get free again. It was only a matter of time.

But the stranger must have anticipated this move.

"Halt," he commanded. Without removing his sword from my throat, he tossed a short rope at me. "Loop that around your wrists, behind your back."

I sighed. "I won't run."

He laughed humorlessly. "I'm not that stupid. Now do as I say."

A strange compulsion came over me, and I was halfway to finishing the job before I realized what I was doing.

What the hell was wrong with me?

"Hurry up," he barked. A strange but pleasant sensation came over me, a gentle urging to comply.

No, I thought, and the feeling lifted.

Did this man know magic of his own? Was he also part siren?

He must have grown tired of waiting because he removed the sword from my neck and grabbed the rope. One tug, and I would have been secure, but I wasn't about to let that happen.

I pulled away, letting the rope drop. He reached for me, raising his blade, and I ducked under it. But instead of running away, I charged him, driving my shoulder straight into his gut. Caught off guard, he stepped backward. I recovered myself and jammed my knee into his nuts.

He crumpled to the ground with a cry of agony.

I should have run, but that hadn't worked before, so I felt for his dagger. I got it, but he grabbed my arm, and we tussled on the ground. I straddled him, preparing to plunge the blade deep into his flesh. If this was how it had to be, then so be it.

But in a move that I hadn't seen coming, he flipped us over, placing himself between my legs and pinning my body to the ground, his hands pinning mine, along with the blade. I bucked underneath him, trying to flip him over, but he was too heavy.

We were both breathing heavily at this point, and for just a moment, I noticed his bright hazel eyes cloud over, not with anger, but with something else. Like there was a deep well of sadness there. Not that I really cared—I had plenty of my own sorrow to deal with.

"Enough."

This time, I didn't feel a compulsion to obey, but after a few more moments of struggling without results, I stopped, anyway. I was tired, and fighting was getting me nowhere. Better to save my strength to get away at a better opportunity.

I should have been home long ago. Instead, I was lying on the ground with a man on top of me.

My helplessness could have been terrifying, but I

didn't get the sense that he wanted my body. Not like the soldiers had, anyway. Though I hated the stranger right at that moment, the feeling of his body pressed against mine was surprisingly solid and warm, and in other circumstances, I could have enjoyed it.

More than enjoyed it.

At that thought, I began to laugh. The man in black looked puzzled, and it only made me laugh harder. Here I was, about to die, my best friend murdered, and I was thinking about sex. It was absurd.

"I can still bind you," he said, ignoring my outburst, "but I would prefer not to. Give me your word you won't sing or run, and I'll let you stand."

I snorted in laughter. "I believe we are at an impasse. Because I have nothing to tell you, and since you have nothing to gain from me, you're just as likely to kill me when you find out I can't help you. So go ahead and do it now so I don't have to walk anymore."

"I'm not in the habit of killing helpless women, even if you would kill me."

Heat warmed my cheeks, and I was glad he couldn't see it in the dark. I *had* tried to kill him, hadn't I? And I knew without a doubt that given the chance, I'd try again if I felt threatened. "Do I look helpless to you? Aside from our current position, I mean."

The man in black gazed into my eyes for a moment and then shook his head. "I'm looking for information, not more bloodshed. Tell me what you were doing on that road, and I will consider your tale, to see if I find you trustworthy."

"And yet I've already proven that I am not."

"Infuriating woman," he growled. "I'm trying to find a way out of this predicament that won't involve one of us being dead. And if you value your life—"

But he didn't complete his thought, and my hearing tuned into what had interrupted him.

Horses.

CHAPTER FIVE

We both froze and listened, but no one approached; the soldiers hadn't heard our argument, then. There was no doubt about their identity. Weapons and armor made a distinct sound when they were on horseback.

The man in black slowly slid off me but motioned for me to stay low. I rolled my eyes. It wasn't like I was going to jump up and shout for the hunters to come save me.

"If you value your life at all, you'll follow me and do exactly as I say," he whispered.

I scowled. "What makes you think I trust you more than I trust any of them?"

But the mysterious man was already sliding away through the tall grass. It barely parted for him, as if he were nothing more than a mouse scurrying through the fields.

With the soldiers closing in, I couldn't stay out in the open, so I followed him. He obviously didn't want to get captured, either, considering he'd slain a Deviant and his guards.

Moonlight bathed the black-clad soldiers on horses, branching out to search. They must have found the massacre by the wagons and followed my trail, somehow, though it should have been impossible. I would have blamed it on the man in black, except I could barely see where he was going, and he was right in front of me. He had some skill in hiding, it seemed, and I wondered when and how he had learned it.

I wasn't quite as stealthy, but I knew how to keep quiet. Inevitably, the grass moved as I passed, and I paused frequently to make sure riders weren't bearing down on my location. Finally, I saw my mystery man's boot go over the side of the river bank. I followed, sliding down into the mud. At the bottom, he grabbed my arm and pulled me, hunched over, to a place where the land kicked out over the water, where the water had eroded the soil and created a shallow overhang. It was as good a place to hide as any, especially now that we were camou-flaged with mud.

A group of soldiers brought their horses to the river to drink. One of those men decided to walk out onto the overhang, and a stream of piss shot out over us into the water.

"Hey, Henrik," came a gruff voice. The man above us finished his business and grunted. Presumably his name was Henrik.

"This siren is leading us on a wild goose chase," said the other man. "And I'm getting tired of chasing her all over these cursed lands."

"It's not your job to be tired of anything," said Henrik in an annoyed voice. "All we got to do is follow the captain, kill the witch and her cronies, and get back to our cups. I got my eye on a wench at that tavern we passed a few days ago."

"And yet you're not to get her, are you, not until we find this bitch."

I held my breath, shifting just a bit to hear the conversation over the flow of the water. The man in black had stilled with his hand on my arm, but he was apparently listening as well.

"What is it she's stolen, anyway," said the second man. "Better be some great jewel after all this trouble."

"It's better than that," Henrik said.

"You mean you know what it is?"

"Aye." Hendrik lowered his voice until I had to strain to hear. "Rumor says it's the horn of an alicorn."

"What's an alicorn?"

"Magical creature," said Henrik cryptically.

"You're about as helpful as a rash on me ass. What *kind* of magical creature?"

"And you're about as useful as a fart on an ant. What's the point of you knowin', anyway?"

"And what's the point of you, at all? Why do you need to know, and I don't, yeah? The way I figure it, we're both out here in the armpit of the country, doin' the same thing." He spit loudly. "Smells like an armpit too."

There was no talking for a moment, and then Henrik relented, sounding smug. "An alicorn is like a unicorn, but with dragon wings and fangs. You don't want to get tangled up with one, not without a mage or two with you.

Its horn is the most dangerous part of it, and the most valuable."

His companion laughed. "That's a load of shite. Ain't no such thing."

"Shut your trap, it's true. I heard the mage talk about it before he went away and got himself killed. They say the beast was caught far south of here. And it killed a company of men before they were able to subdue it and slaughter it. And now, its horn is being sent to The Harrow. So we're on important business for The Harrow himself, and you better stop asking questions so we can get to findin' that witch. Snow's coming before morning."

There was a loud noise as the other man slapped his leg. "All the better, I say. That way she won't be able to go nowhere without tracks."

"You really have nothing in that big lumpy head of yours, do you?" said Henrik. "After the snowstorm, sure, but it'd be damn hard to find her in the middle of one, and that's if we don't freeze first. I'd rather keep my balls than have them frozen over before I find that wench."

The two men went off laughing. As they retreated, the puzzle pieces began to fall into place, and I sat thinking about what I'd heard.

Alicorns were extremely rare; almost no one had ever seen one. In fact, just like the second man, most people thought they were myths to frighten villagers into submission. It was said that the kings of old all had alicorns in their stables, and that they'd use them on the peasants if there was any unrest. My mother had told me many stories when I was young, and the tale of the alicorn was one of them.

The creatures were generally shaped liked horses, but they had fangs instead of teeth, claws instead of hooves, and leathery scales instead of a hide. And they were vicious. I didn't doubt for one minute that it had taken an entire company of The Harrow's soldiers to bring one down.

The reason for everything was becoming clear. An alicorn horn was an extremely rare item, with multiple magical uses. That explained why there had been a mage, and why they were prepared for thieves. They couldn't risk the alicorn horn being stolen. And yet... they had failed, though it wasn't my fault.

If I had known what was in the package, I would have gone straight to it instead of worrying about the gold. Then maybe Flint and I would have gotten away. Silently cursing my rotten luck, I scowled at the man in black. He was obviously after the horn and thought I knew its location, which was why the soldiers were still looking for me, as well. I was their main target.

Did the soldiers think I had killed that mage and all his men? With a shudder, I realized I was now an enormous danger to my family. While these soldiers were hunting me, I could never go home.

And then, an old memory was triggered. Something my mother had once told me. There was another story... a tale about grinding an alicorn horn into powder and using it for a special brew. The brew was said to be potent, even deadly. To some creatures, anyway. But there was an understanding that if a human was cursed, then the brew would kill the curse inside them.

It could even change who a person was. It could remove the siren in my blood.

Or Laney's blood. The very idea was starting to make my heart hammer inside my chest. It could be the answer to all our problems. If we were human, *completely* human, then we could live anywhere, work anywhere.

I could rip out the beast inside me that had caused so much harm, that had brought me so much hate. I could give Laney a chance at a normal life, or whatever passed for normal these days.

With a twinge of guilt, I remembered my sister's trusting, too-big eyes, and her tiny, webbed hands. I would miss those. And I felt a flare of hate for the intolerant assholes who made being ourselves a mortal danger.

But if it meant she wouldn't be hunted, and she had a chance to live, what choice did I have? If I could change it, I should want to. I certainly had no reservations about changing myself.

In the meantime, we couldn't have been more than a mile from home, and it wouldn't take much searching for the soldiers to find my family. I couldn't let them keep looking, not here.

I needed to draw the soldiers away. Quickly, I slid toward the water.

The man in black caught my arm. "Where the hell are you going?"

"To create a diversion," I whispered.

"From what?"

"If you want to find out, then you'll have to follow."

Without another word, I slipped from his grasp and slid into the water without making a sound. Pushing past the shock of cold, I smiled as I moved out of his reach. He could have fought me, but then we would have blown our cover.

I knew this river for miles in any direction, and here it flowed swiftly. I took a deep breath and plunged under the water, quickly pulling myself into the middle, where it was deepest.

There was no point in looking back—either the warrior in black would follow, or he wouldn't. I pulled myself along the bottom, letting the current carry me and using my hands to avoid crashing into larger rocks.

There was a stream of something warm that stung my eyes, and I tried not to gag when I thought about the soldier pissing in the river.

My lungs were bursting long before it was safe to surface, but I held my breath, relaxing and letting the cold water carry me far away. When I finally felt the spasms getting ready to take over, I flipped over and surfaced, letting my mouth and nose leave the water but nothing else.

Snowflakes were drifting lazily through the night air. I risked a glance back. The horses and the soldiers were out of sight, and there had been no cry of alarm, no crossbow bolts piercing the water. They hadn't seen me.

But I needed them to know in which direction I was heading. Cupping my hand to my mouth, I let out a high-pitched shriek, as if I'd been mortally wounded. I listened, and when I didn't hear anything, repeated the noise. Finally, shouts sounded from far off.

Then I glanced at the water. Something was floating upstream. The stranger in black. Maybe he was dead. I couldn't tell in the dark, but my life would be easier if he was.

With a pang of guilt and grief, I turned and left my family behind. After creating a diversion, I had to hide for a few days. I couldn't risk leading anyone back to the village, and the only consolation was that Rose would look after Laney and my father while she waited for Flint, who would never come home.

The current accelerated, and I banged up against a few rocks that I didn't see in time. They jolted me out of my thoughts, and I looked around. I'd traveled farther than I'd thought; the rapids must be ahead.

Finding a landing place, I snared a tree branch along the shore and pulled myself onto the bank.

As much as I wanted to rest, I watched the water for signs of the man in black. Finally, I saw a dark shape drifting on the surface, and then a head. He was looking for me.

I hesitated before signaling him. I didn't want him to follow me, but he would see my diversion, anyway. No point in letting him out of my sight just yet, and I could use his help. He saw me and swam to the bank with powerful strokes. When he pulled himself up next to me, he was barely out of breath.

"You didn't die," I said as if it surprised me. It did, a little.

"Sorry to disappoint," he said. "Why are we creating a diversion? We lost them."

"Like I'd tell *you*." I hurried into a dense thicket, and he followed.

"What do you have in mind?" he asked. "Fire?"

"No." I scrambled onto a crop of boulders and shrieked again. "A special skill of mine," I said, grinning at his stunned look. The shriek wasn't magic, but for some reason lost to time, Flint and I used to practice screaming bloody murder. We were kids with nothing but chores to do and no toys to play with. It was always a contest, and I always won. We'd kept up the game until we got old enough to realize how dangerous it was, and that there was always something or someone listening.

I slid off my boulder and moved upward, where the horses couldn't follow. Finding another boulder, I climbed to the top and kept a lookout, shivering. There was only room for one person, and I chose it intentionally to keep the stranger away.

He didn't get the hint, however, and soon climbed up to crouch beside me, too close for comfort.

"Go find your own place to haunt."

"I'm not letting you out of my sight," he said. "You've already wasted my entire day, and I'm not going to spend what's left of the night chasing you down again."

"Then don't. I don't have the alicorn horn, and I don't know where it is. That's what you're after, isn't it?"

My companion didn't say anything.

"Thought so," I said smugly. "Why do you want it?"

But he didn't answer, and we lapsed into an awkward silence while we listened for the soldiers.

It was an hour before I heard horses' hooves, but I didn't wait for a glimpse of them before climbing down. I intentionally made some noise by breaking a few branches, and then I shrieked one more time for good measure. This time, voices rang out. I froze. They were much closer than I'd anticipated.

"Shit," I whispered, and then I began scrambling over the rocks toward the forest.

The ground was mostly rocky with thorny vines, forcing me to alternate climbing and running until the boulders turned into rocky bluffs. Above the soldiers, where the horses couldn't follow.

If I thought the man in black would have trouble, I was surprised. True to his word, my new shadow didn't lose sight of me for an instant. He stole through the night like a cat on the prowl, making no noise. I had never seen someone walk so stealthily and thought that in another life, he would have been useful on my runs with Flint.

If he weren't so stubborn and infuriating.

Every few minutes, I'd make some obvious noise, wanting to give the soldiers something to chase. And each time, they seemed to get closer.

"What did they do?" I asked. "Put wings on their horses?"

"They are hunters, not mere soldiers, and they are patient. They know we have to come down sometime."

THE NIGHT WORE ON, and my body began to protest all the mistreatment. It had been more than a day since I had slept, and between having my best friend murdered, being captured, and then trying to lead hunters away from my village, I was exhausted. I didn't think I could go any farther without sleep. The man in black didn't even look tired.

Even after several hours of scrambling over rocks, my clothes were still wet, and a chill had set in. I longed for a good, hot fire, but something urged me to keep going. A strong feeling that the soldiers were close.

With a cold chill that had nothing to do with my clothes, I realized it was possible they had another mage with them.

If there had been one with the first company, then there could be one with the second, and their tracking skills, aided by magic, were more than enough to find the likes of me. Up here, the wind chilled me to the bone, and there was no shelter to be found. The man in black had been right—we had to come down sometime. Or light a fire, or sleep.

And then we would be caught.

I was starting to resign myself to my fate when my companion spoke for the first time in several hours. "I know a cave not far from here. We can hole up and get a few hours' sleep."

As the first light tipped the rocks above us with a golden glow, he led me toward a wooded area, lower than I liked, but rockier. A dried-up stream had formed a narrow ravine, hidden from view until one came upon it. We followed it for some time.

Finally, he turned aside and ducked into a small hole beneath two large boulders leaning together. I followed, having to bend double and then belly crawl to follow him inside. But the short tunnel soon opened into a rather large dry cave. Bits of light leaked through gaps in the stone above, just enough to show the faint outlines of rock.

Wood was piled off the side—someone had spent time here before, and I assumed it was my stranger in black, though why he would have been hiding here was a mystery.

He started a fire that soon threw flickering shadows on the wall. There was no smoke, and the heat felt glorious on my numb fingers and cheeks.

"We stay for now," my companion said quietly. "Feel free to get some sleep. I'll make sure no one disturbs you."

I wasn't ready to just fall asleep just like that. My mind was racing with the events of the day before, and despite my fatigue, my brain was replaying Flint's death over and over. Now that I had stopped moving, I couldn't shut out the thoughts of his fall, his headless body. It took everything I had not to break down and cry in front of this man I didn't know.

But mostly, I thought about what it would be like to put the soldiers into an enchanted sleep and then set the forest on fire around them. Leaving them for the flames seemed like a just choice. I didn't care where the soldiers were from, only that they had done nothing but cause me and my family misery. After a while, I even voiced these thoughts.

He listened calmly but then eventually shook his head. "It's one thing to kill someone in battle, and another entirely to not give them a fighting chance."

"We all die, stranger, but sometimes justice is best when served on a platter of painful vengeance."

He said nothing, still staring into the fire. "Believe it

or not," he said finally, "I have felt similar wrath. And I've also learned that a person's death cannot be measured by the scales of justice. Trying to do so would make you go mad."

I laughed, but there was no humor in it. "Then I have long been mad, so what's the harm in going a little madder?"

"To some, life means little or nothing. But to me, either all life means something, or it can mean nothing at all. I can't look at it both ways."

I scoffed and brought my knees up under my chin. "You have high ideals, stranger, especially for a man who doesn't hesitate to kill when you want to."

"There have been times I've served justice at the end of my blade, true, but do I want to? Not necessarily."

"Justice is nothing but a rich man's way of pretending to care," I said finally. "Because we all know how the world really works."

"Ah. A true cynic," he said with a smile turning one corner of his mouth.

I shrugged. "I call it like I see it."

The man laughed a little and nodded. But then he didn't say anything else for a while.

Finally, I couldn't ignore the obvious any longer. "Tell me about the alicorn horn."

I knew of the myths and fables surrounding them, knew of the creatures that possessed them and how rare they were. If an alicorn horn had truly been stolen, it was no wonder there were soldiers and mages looking for it.

The man in black studied me a moment before

seeming to decide something. "One was killed south of here, and now the world is in great peril."

I scoffed. "The world has always been in great peril. Why is it worse now?"

He stared into the fire and didn't answer.

"You still think I have it?" I asked indignantly. "If I had, I wouldn't have stayed with you these last few miles. I would have made sure the soldiers found you and then been on my way."

"You think you could do that? You think you would have been able to leave me there for the soldiers to find?"

He had a point. I might have tried, but he was crafty, and more intelligent than I'd given him credit for at first. "I could have lost you on the trail miles ago."

He nodded. "Maybe. But that doesn't mean you didn't have anything to do with the horn's disappearance. If it weren't for you, I might have found it already and been gone without anyone being the wiser."

"What do you want to do with it?" I asked in exasperation. "And why pick that spot to steal it?"

"I only learned about it two days ago and caught up to the trail about the same time you did. My reasons are my own, and as far as I'm concerned, you can fuck off with your righteous indignation. If you weren't there for the alicorn horn, what were you there for?"

"I was there for the shipment of goods, to take care of my family. I found the gold shipment instead."

He snorted. "That wasn't a shipment of gold, just what a company of soldiers carry with them from time to time. You expect me to believe that you were after such a small sum?" He stood and towered over me, glaring down at me. I stood as well.

I was stunned that he could think so little of life-saving coin. We were obviously from two different worlds. "That gold could have kept us alive for the next year, could have bought bread for the entire village!"

I thought about putting him to sleep right there and running. But I was tired, too tired. Instead, I turned away from him and sat with my back to the cave wall.

"Should've tied you up and left you when I had the chance," I muttered.

"The feeling is mutual. You say you don't have it. I'm prepared to believe you, but don't do that trick with your voice again. Agreed?"

I studied him, looking at the firelight reflected in his eyes, trying to decide what kind of man I thought he was, if I was safe. He was obviously high born, or at least hadn't known hardship, and I didn't trust that. But he could have killed me ten times over, and he hadn't. My gut told me I could at least get some sleep, but I didn't trust that, either. My body was fighting for sleep; it wanted me to give in. My mind was aware this man had bested an entire company of soldiers on his own, and though he hadn't killed me, I wasn't sure of his reasons for keeping me alive.

"What?" he asked.

"I don't trust you," I said.

"And I don't trust you."

"But you have all the weapons."

"I wouldn't disqualify that singing of yours. It's weapon enough."

I stared pointedly at his dagger. With a sigh, he unfastened the dagger from his belt and tossed it to me along with the sheath. "There. In case you ever feel threatened, I give you permission to drive that blade into my heart. All I want is what I came for and nothing else. But I tell you this—you can sleep without worry. Nothing in this cave wishes you harm."

The dagger was symbolic, I knew. I'd seen the way he wielded that sword. But it was something, and I felt better for having it. I put it on my belt and nodded.

He sat, finally, on the opposite side of the fire, and we sat in mutual dislike for a long time, me fighting sleep against the wall, and him staring into the fire as if it held the answer to all his problems. Despite my resolve to stay awake, sleep took me before I even knew my eyes were closed. I didn't know how long I slept before I jerked awake. Despite the fire, the cave was cold, and the stranger sat in the same position, making me think I'd only dozed for a moment.

"Now that we've both had a bit of sleep," he said finally, "let's chat."

I straightened against the cave wall and rubbed my eyes. How long *had* I been asleep? The daylight filtering through the rocks above us had changed to the opposite wall. So, I had slept at least a few hours, perhaps all morning.

"Chat about what?" I asked.

"If there's anything you need, I'll do my best to provide it, in exchange for what you know about the alicorn horn."

I shook my head. "I don't have any more information." But if I did, I'd look for the horn myself, I thought.

He stood, the irritation plain on his face, and seemed to be prepared to say something biting, but he didn't get the chance.

At that moment, a sound came from deeper within the cave, and we both turned toward it. It was a half-hiss, half-growl, hard to describe and yet obviously dangerous. The hair on my arms stood on end. And then, in the flicker of the firelight, I saw the outline of a horse-sized monster squeeze through a narrow crack in the rocks and land on the floor of the cave in front of us.

The monster had eight legs and two heads, each at the end of stalks, like a snail but with too many eyes to count, and a whip-like tail that looked as if it could take my head off with one swipe.

And that's exactly what it tried to do. I ducked and flung myself to the cave floor as I tracked the song of my companion's sword. Metal cracked on flesh, but no sound of blood or screech of pain. I hadn't noticed the monster's armor because I'd been too busy being terrified by all its other horrible features.

The man in black cursed and rolled to the side to avoid a slash from that razor-like tail. Attempting to avoid the fire or getting pinned to the wall, I scrambled to my feet and backed away from the fight.

And what a fight it was. The warrior was staving off the monster's attempts to behead him with its tail, and slashing whenever he got the opportunity.

Then, I saw jaws appear at the end of each stalk, weird

things that had been hidden before. The creature was able to move these appendages independently, and so not only did the warrior have to dodge swipes of the tail, but also needle-like fangs that reached out to bite his face off.

My companion was hacking away at the beast, moving as if he was fully rested. Steadily, he drove the creature back. I had my dagger in hand, but no idea how I was going to strike the monster without getting hurt. I was good with a blade, but not that good.

Instead, knowing I would feel shame about it later, I ducked my head and crawled through the hole. When I emerged on the other side, the sun had reached its zenith and was already heading toward the mountains to the west. From within the cave came the clash of steel on armor, and I hesitated. But really, what was I supposed to do?

I had seen that man take on more than a dozen soldiers and a mage at the same time; he could handle a single monster.

So, I ran.

CHAPTER SIX

Hungry and exhausted, I made my way back to the place where I figured I could find food. Not home because there was no food there, and I was sure the soldiers hadn't given up their search.

Back to the wagons. I didn't know where else to go. It took the rest of the afternoon, and more than once I thought I was being followed. But when no one appeared, I kept moving.

Stopping would mean sleeping. And sleeping could mean death. Out here without shelter, without protection other than a dagger, I would be easy prey for the monsters, not to mention the soldiers.

When I finally reached the wagons, the bodies were still there. The dead soldiers had all been left where they had fallen. The man in black had said they were dead when he found them, but I wasn't so sure. Unless the same person who had stolen the alicorn horn had also killed these men.

Carrion birds were already picking at the bodies, and

there were growls of scavengers fighting over carcasses under the trees.

Ignoring the sounds, I began ransacking the wagons for food. I found some cheese and stuffed it into my mouth while I looked for anything else that was valuable. I found a crossbow and a few bolts. I had never used one before, but it could replace my lost bow in a pinch. I spent a few minutes struggling to load the bolt into the bow and arm it, but after a lot of cursing and pain, I managed.

More scavengers were showing up, and I watched the birds circle overhead. I thought of Flint's body, unprotected from the foul creatures, and I almost lost the food I'd just eaten. Instead of worrying about it, I began gathering large rocks.

He might never be able to go home, but I could raise a cairn, at least. And while I worked, I formed a plan. By the time the sun was once again setting, I had covered Flint's body. He was safe from scavengers, anyway. I wiped the tears from my cheeks, cursed the human monsters who had killed him, and said a final goodbye.

Picking up the crossbow, I turned, planning on hiding somewhere for a few hours' rest. It was only then that I saw the man in black, standing a few paces behind me.

"You!" I said, raising the crossbow and pointing it at him. "Why do you keep following me? Haven't you had enough?"

I couldn't believe it. Out of all the foolish things... Did he really think I knew where the alicorn horn was?

Forget singing. I thought about shooting him right there. But then I saw how pale his face was, and the sweat dripping off him. Blood coated his right shoulder, and he held his arm tight to his side.

I had been so sure of myself, so sure that I could get away from him. Since I couldn't risk going home yet, I had planned to arm myself from the dead soldiers and then try to find the trail of the true thief. Even though I had no lead, it was the only thing I could think of to do. If I found the alicorn horn, maybe our luck would change—maybe it would have all been worth it.

A loud voice in my head said nothing would be worth Flint's death, but I couldn't go back home, not yet, especially with this stranger dogging my footsteps. I opened my mouth to sing, with plans to leave him behind for good.

And then, to my extreme annoyance, the man in black took one step toward me and fell flat on his face.

Was he faking?

I walked over to him but stopped outside of arm's length. He didn't seem like the type of guy to play dead, but a girl could never be too careful. He was breathing, but it was labored, and then I saw the severity of the wound on his arm.

I gently rolled him over onto his back and examined it.

Something had pierced his upper arm, driving all the way through muscle to the bone. And it was already green with pus—venom, I was sure. He must have been injured fighting that monster.

What was I supposed to do now? He would need a poultice and a tea, for sure, and maybe even something else.

But I didn't have time for this. I had to find the person who had the alicorn horn. It could save my family.

And yet... I couldn't leave him there to die. That's what would happen if he didn't get help soon.

Suddenly, I felt bad for leaving him in the cave to face the monster alone, even if I couldn't have done anything. I owed him, dammit. He had saved me from the soldiers.

"Damn it all to fucking hell," I grumbled.

I looked into his pale face and reached out to touch the line of his square jaw, covered in days-old stubble. Even when closed, his eyes were beautiful, with long dark lashes and eyebrows that weren't too bushy—I never liked bushy eyebrows on a man.

I sighed. "You win, stranger. You win."

As I grasped him under the shoulders and began to drag him toward the cover of the trees, I tried not to think about what I would have done if he'd been ugly. I suppose I would have done the same thing, but at least he was pleasant to look at, especially now that he had passed out.

Every bone and muscle in my body screamed with the effort, but somehow I managed to move him. It took a long time, and it wasn't just because of my own injuries. With all the dead bodies, the flies flew over my head in swarms, and I had to stop and shoo them away from his arm several times. By the time I reached the safety of the trees, my back and legs ached, and I was so far past the point of exhaustion there wasn't even a word for how I felt. How I got him into the forest, I didn't know, but once he was there, I couldn't waste any time.

I removed his armor and set it aside. Though I knew little about such things, it seemed well-made, and it may have saved his life. There were plenty of scratches on the leather, signs of previous battles, and a long, ragged scratch where something had pierced his shoulder. If it hadn't been for his armor, the man might have lost his arm. And likely his life.

The shirt beneath was soaked with blood, and I removed that, too. I was surprised to find a large tattoo on the left side of his chest—a raven in flight. It was beautifully done, but there was no time to wonder about its significance. The wound was covered in blood and sticky, black goo, and it stank.

Laying him down on a bed of springy earth with his head and chest elevated, I began searching for what I needed. The forest was a treasure trove of herbs and plants, and while I didn't know as much as my mother had, I'd learned plenty over the years about caring for the sick and injured.

And I'd seen enough injuries and death to know what could be fixed and what couldn't. I thought this stranger could be fixed, so I had to try.

"Don't you dare die while I'm gone," I said as I left him beside the tree, hidden in a little hollow.

I found everything I needed, despite the deepening darkness, despite my weariness. The last thing I found was some belladonna, growing ominously beneath the shade of a large tree. Carefully removing some, I took it back to my stranger.

He was still breathing. A good enough sign that he was tough and might live, after all. After building a small fire, I ran back to the wagons, fighting the flies to look for a bowl or mortar and pestle. I found a small iron pot, round and shaped like a cauldron, perfect for brewing.

When I returned, the stranger was breathing more shallowly, and for a moment, I thought he'd stopped altogether. But then I watched his chest and saw him take another ragged breath.

Quickly, I began crushing and shredding herbs, which I dropped into the bottom of the cauldron. Luckily, I'd found a stream for water and added it to the pot. It wasn't going to be my finest work, but I didn't have much time. Finally, I ripped up my shirtsleeve to act as a bandage. Then I dipped the fabric into the liquid of the cauldron, soaking up the mixture that had boiled down into a gel-like goo not unlike the sticky substance that was smeared over his clothing.

I coated his wound, burning my fingers in my haste. Washing his arm in the spring under a new moon would have been preferable, but we were weeks away from that, and he didn't have that much time.

With a deep breath, I began wrapping the scalding poultice around his upper arm and shoulder. He woke then, his eyes flying open in a hiss of pain as it scalded his skin.

"Hold still," I said. "It'll feel better soon."

I wrapped the fabric all the way around, making sure

to cover the tendrils of poison that were already creeping up his arm, beneath the skin. The man slumped back into unconsciousness as I tied off the makeshift bandage. I covered him with his heavy cloak and then began tending the camp.

Adding wood to the fire was the next priority, and though it could bring the soldiers, I was pretty confident that we left them far behind. And it really didn't matter if we hadn't. Without the fire, this man would die. I knew it in my bones, just as I knew that he had earned my help. So I watched and waited. At one point, I brewed some tea for myself, something that would alleviate the swelling in my jaw.

I sat with him all night, checking on him every few minutes, with one break to get food. Because it was the simplest, I went back to the wagons, where I found a jug of wine and some more hard cheese, along with a few other bits of food that wouldn't spoil. I stuffed them into my mouth while I loaded up my shirt with more. I also found some other supplies that I had missed earlier, including a change of clothes and boots for me, a tattered cloak that was just short enough for me to wear, a different shirt for the stranger, and a large pack. Loading up the pack, I trudged back to the campsite, feeling like a wrung-out rag.

The cheese assuaged my hunger, and the wine was strong. I drank until a tingle began in my head and my body was warm. Then I put the stopper in and saved the rest for later. Beyond a few moans and groans, the man in black remained unconscious, but his breathing became easier as the poultice did its job. Hopefully, it would counteract the venom in the wound and begin to draw it out. By morning, I would remove the bandage, and with it, the worst of the toxin.

I'd never dressed anything as severe before, but the concept was the same. If the monster had bitten his arm off, I wouldn't have been able to fix it, but as soon as I pulled out the venom and the infection, I could stitch the wound and keep it clean.

The wine and food had made me sleepy, and as he began to breathe easier, I allowed myself to doze sitting up against a tree. When the first tendrils of light broke between the leaves, I brewed a tea over the fire using a tin cup I had found at the wagons. Then, I let it cool just enough before tipping it into the stranger's mouth.

I lifted his head and dribbled some of it over his lips. His eyes fluttered open, saw the drink, and began to sip. His lips were dry, and I imagined he was incredibly thirsty. He said nothing as I helped him drink, his arms useless at his side. Finally, when the tea was finished, I set down the cup and began to remove the bandage.

The smell was foul, and I retched a couple of times while taking it off. It was soaked in fresh blood and venom, but the wound looked clear. I thanked the stars and then tossed the bandage into the fire. Then I threaded a thick needle, the finest one I had found, and began to sew. The tea had a numbing effect, and though I heard a few moans, I purposely didn't look to see if my stranger was awake. I was trying not to lose my nerve as I sewed the large wounds on both sides of his arm and shoulder.

The skin was scalded, and those burns would be

painful over the next few days. But they would heal cleanly, and that was all I could wish for right now. When I finished stitching him up, I gave him a long drink of the wine. This time, he was able to lift the jug with his good arm. He took a long swig, the red liquid pouring down the sides of his face.

"Easy there, killer," I said, taking it away from him. "Don't drown yourself just as you're coming around to the living."

He took a breath and then wiped his chin, his face still pale but not the deathly gray it had been last night. He swallowed, tried to sit up, and then winced in pain. I put a hand on his chest and pushed him back down gently.

"In a hurry to go somewhere?"

"You really are a witch," he rasped. "What have you done to my legs?"

I shook my head. "Not a witch, just a concerned passerby. And your legs are feeling the effects of the tea. I couldn't have you wiggling around while I was sewing you up. The sensation will fade in a minute."

He relaxed a bit, his body sagging against the moss as he took a few steadying breaths. They were strong, and his color was improving every minute. He was going to live.

"You saved me," he said matter-of-factly.

I shrugged. "I figured it was my fault you got hurt, and I owed you."

He shook his head slightly. "It wasn't your fault. We had no way of knowing that beast was in there.

Although... If you had stuck around with my dagger, maybe you could have distracted it while I killed it."

I glared at him, but then saw the side of his mouth work up into a smirk.

"You killed it, then?" I asked.

"Yes."

"Guess you didn't need my distraction after all. There's food. Are you hungry?"

He moved around a little more and then winced. "Yes, but I... may need help."

"Are you sure you're not just playing? Because I'm not a nurse, you know."

"Trust me, it hurts my pride to ask you to feed me just as much as I'm sure it hurts your pride to do it."

Fair enough. I helped him to a sitting position and propped some supplies behind his back, including the large pack that was going to replace the satchel I'd lost. I tried not to think about the circumstances of that loss, not just then.

I helped him eat, letting him finish the rest of the cheese. By the time he was done, his color had fully returned.

"What do you know," I said. "You're going to live, stranger."

"And now I have to leave."

I laughed. "You're not going anywhere just yet. You almost died."

He sat forward on his own, wincing with the effort but already looking stronger. "I need to find that trail before it grows completely cold."

"Get this through your head—you're in no shape to travel."

"How convenient for you. I suppose it'll give you a head start," he said wryly. "Thinking of leaving me here to fend for myself while I get better?"

I shook my head. "I said you were going to live, not that you can live by yourself. You're going to need to drink a tea four times a day until you're mended."

"Another tea. And are you going to tell me how to make it?"

"Sure, but you're in no shape to gather the ingredients yourself. Not yet. And it's a tricky brew. Not just anyone can throw the ingredients into the pot and get the same result I do."

The sun was streaming through the forest leaves and lighting his dark hair. "So you are a witch. Or you were raised by one?"

He was fishing, but I didn't take the bait. "I'm not a witch, so you don't need to worry about your precious blood or whatever else you're worried about me taking. If I wanted to use you as a sacrifice to all my favorite gods and goddesses, I would have done that already."

"So what gives you the gift, then?" he said. "That song had power."

I began gathering all the things and putting them into the pack. It was going to be as long as my torso when I got done, but I figured I could manage it.

"You aren't completely human, are you?" he prodded.

I ignored him, pretending to be interested in the pack.

"Are you part songbird—a very scary songbird?" he asked rhetorically. "I don't see any feathers, though it would explain the beautiful voice. Though not the power within it."

I smothered the fire and watched the embers die. "It's not important that you know."

"Maybe not, but I'm curious. When you sing, you can enchant people into sleep, a rare gift. If you're not a songbird, and not a witch, maybe it's something else. A siren, perhaps? Though you don't look like one."

"And how would you know what a siren looks like?"

He shrugged, then winced at the pain. "In case you're worried, I don't care what you are." He pinned me with a stare. "I only know that you've saved my life, and I'm grateful. More than you could know."

I scoffed. "You don't care, huh? Do you have some kind of weird kink? A fetish for half-breeds, perhaps?"

"I would never call you that, and why do you want to know my kinks?"

"I don't."

"You just asked, so I assumed—" A slight smile curved the corners of his mouth.

Glaring at him, I stood. "Guess you'll have to fend for yourself then, if you're going to make fun of me."

The stranger lost his smile and held up his good hand as if to stop me. "Just a bit of teasing, but I'm sorry. You don't know me and I don't know you."

I paused. "You're right, but it shouldn't bother me like it does. Let's just say that after that run-in with the Deviant, I'm feeling a bit raw."

"Understandable." He sobered even more and regarded me with a look that I couldn't decipher, but a small understanding seemed to pass between us, anyway. "Look, am I going to be able to walk anytime soon?"

"Soon, yeah. You could try standing now."

He didn't waste any time. In a few moments, he was hesitantly on his feet, swaying a little but gaining strength every second. "Where's my shirt?"

I had been trying not to stare at his lean muscles, at the way they rippled when he moved, and almost jumped at the question. Had he caught me looking? I swallowed and practically shoved the borrowed shirt into his chest, then hastily removed my hand. "I burned your old one."

"It'll do," he said, pulling it gingerly over his head. He couldn't get it over his bad shoulder, however, so I had to help him. Then I helped put his armor back on, as well. I couldn't carry it, and he said he didn't want to leave it. He winced when it touched his shoulder but otherwise didn't complain.

Finally, I slung the large pack over my shoulders. It was heavy, but not enough to slow me down. I had packed the remainder of the tea ingredients on top. Unfortunately, it required a fresh brewing every time, so I couldn't simply make it ahead of time and carry with me.

"I don't expect you to do any more than you've already done," the man said, his good hand resting on the pommel of the sword, which he had transferred to his other hip. "Tell me how to brew the tea, and I'll leave you alone. It's the least I can do."

"You don't think I'm after your precious prize?"

"I know now if you had been, you wouldn't have stuck around to take care of me." He sounded contrite enough, and my anger at the accusation had leaked out over the night of watching to see if he would live.

I nodded. If our positions were reversed, I would have thought the same thing. "As for the tea, it contains potent and dangerous ingredients. I'm not going to nurse you back to health only to have you poison yourself from brewing it wrong. The only way you'll survive is if I help you, for a time, anyway."

"Except I have an errand that will not wait," he said. He moved around cautiously, like an elderly man who was unsure of his footsteps. "I'm afraid the trail has gone cold, but if I can pick it up again, I will. The true thief could be leagues away by now."

I bit my lip. He couldn't survive on his own, and I couldn't go home, not if there was even a chance of leading soldiers back there. And the alicorn horn intrigued me, more than a little. I had thought about it all night. If I could get it... if I could use it, Laney's life could be so different than it was now. My life would be different. We wouldn't have to be in hiding.

"Listen," I said. "What if I have an idea about the location of the alicorn horn?" His expression darkened, and I hurried to explain. "I don't know where it is, but I know where you can start looking."

After a moment, he nodded. "At this point, any information could be helpful, but I cannot ask you to help me."

I sniffed. "Maybe I have to. You saved my life, and I realize that now."

"Then we're even."

"Not yet. Trust me, once that tea wears off fully, you'll barely be able to stand again."

"What's your name?"

"Samara. And..." I hesitated. "I do have siren blood in my veins. My great-grandmother."

I waited for him to look at me in disgust, wondering why I'd felt the need to tell him. Maybe I'd hoped it would drive him away so I could go about my business, release me to hate him, somehow.

Instead, he simply nodded. "That's why you can put men into an enchanted sleep."

"And women, though I don't find that they cause quite as much trouble as men. Almost like they welcome a good, dreamless rest."

He barked a laugh and then quickly stifled it.

I waited for him to tell me his name. Finally, he said, "Col."

"A strange name, to me. Where are you from?"

"The North," was all he said, obviously dismissing any further questions.

"If you're coming with me, and I guess you have to because your life is in my hands, Col, we'd better get started. We have a long way to go, and you are going to be exhausted before the end."

He took a halting step. "I'll make it. Whatever speed you set, I will manage."

"You may eat your words later," I said, setting off.

When I glanced back, he was following me, his strides long and sure even though his face had turned pale again.

"You said you knew where to start looking. Where are we going, Samara?"

A small part of me liked the way he said my name. As someone who had always been hated for what I was, I couldn't help but like the way he didn't seem to pass judgment. "Going to a little spot I know, a place called the Thieves' Camp. It's nothing much, except the most obvious place for someone wanting to get rid of stolen goods."

"I've never heard of it."

"And why would you, unless you were a regular thief?"

He didn't speak, confirming my suspicion. This man was not a regular thief, not a common one like me, anyway. He wanted that alicorn horn for something specific, just as I now did. And he had been willing to kill for it.

A piece of information I should not forget.

CHAPTER SEVEN

I pushed the pace as much as I dared, which is to say that we walked faster than a snail, but slower than a tortoise. The trees changed into toothy, rough hills, where we were exposed to frigid air even at midday. The promised snow never materialized, and for that I was grateful. I couldn't imagine trying to cross this terrain while worrying about slipping off the edge of a steep drop-off.

Despite his injury, Col pressed forward, but he stumbled often. He didn't ask to stop, and I didn't suggest it. My own injuries were insignificant compared to his, but I was sore and bruised all over, and my brain kept up a steady tempo against my skull that had nothing to do with the hiking.

Late morning, I stopped to light a small fire in a gap between boulders. Col needed more tea, and I needed to thaw my fingers.

He drank the brew with a grimace.

"That is terrible," he said finally, and I could tell he

was trying not to gag. "Is this something different than I had before?"

"No. But you were at death's door before, so I doubt the taste even registered on your tongue."

He finished gulping it down and then lay back as the effects took hold. The tea still caused him to lose the use of his limbs. Each time he drank, we lost at least an hour.

"Thank you, Samara."

"Why are you being nice to me all of a sudden?" I asked.

"I realize you could have left me at any point after I was injured, but you didn't. I misjudged you."

"I could still leave," I grumbled. "And if you keep thanking me, I will." His gratitude only made me feel guilty for leaving him in the first place. And anyway, we were heading in the same direction, though I wouldn't admit that to Col.

"Where are you from?" I asked again, hoping to get a bit more information than the last time.

"From the north," he repeated cryptically.

"Why are you hunting the alicorn horn?" I asked for the tenth time.

He didn't answer, and instead stared into the sky for a few minutes before shielding his eyes with his left hand. Then, realizing he could move, he sat up and massaged his legs as if to get feeling back into them.

Finally, he spoke. "In the wrong hands, the alicorn horn is a dangerous weapon. As soon as I heard about it, I began going after the shipment. But now I wonder if it was stolen before the carts even began to move, and replaced with a decoy. It could be long gone by now."

"Even if it disappeared days ago, I won't be surprised if we can find some information at the Thieves' Camp. I've never been through there without learning at least one bit of juicy gossip, and an alicorn horn is definitely juicy."

"You're interested in it now, too," he said. "Why?"

"What makes you think I'm interested? I didn't go straight to the Thieves' Camp. I went back to bury my friend."

He shook his head. "Your lies aren't any good on me."

My face flushed in anger. My sole thoughts in returning to the wagons were to make sure Flint was laid to rest, and to find food. I had a chance, and I took it.

Carefully, Col stood and put out the fire. "You have a gift for song, and I have a gift for knowing when someone is telling an untruth."

"But you accused me of stealing the horn and wouldn't listen when I told you the truth. I don't think your skill is as good as *you* think it is."

He laughed, this time without wincing. "Are you going to keep throwing that in my face?"

"You better believe it." I shouldered the bag and began walking. Col followed with a slight chuckle.

By the time darkness came, we left the toothy rocks behind and entered the true foothills of the mountains, climbing ever higher. Each time we crested a hill, I hoped to see the valley I was looking for, and each time, I was disappointed.

"Where are you, dammit?" I muttered. The light was quickly fading, and I didn't want to stumble around this region in the dark. I didn't know it well enough for that.

"Lost?" Col asked, breathing hard and coming up behind me.

"No," I replied brightly. "I know exactly where we are."

"I would suggest we stop and ask for directions, but there don't seem to be any people around. Perhaps it's on the map?"

"We don't need directions, and this isn't on any map." I took a deep, calming breath. Col's not-so-subtle jabs were *not* what I needed. I turned to study him. His face was paler than it had been all day. I was impressed he had lasted this long.

Not that I would tell him that. "You don't look so great," I said. "Time for some tea, and if we do that, we might as well set up a camp for the night." Another night away from home. Hopefully, there wouldn't be too many more.

A flicker of relief crossed his face. "I'm good for a few more hours."

"Goddess give me strength. You are barely standing."

"And you are lost. Admit it."

It wasn't difficult to find a place that was sheltered on three sides. We huddled between some boulders, with just enough room for a small fire. It was a tight space, but it meant we were able to get warm, and most importantly, we were hidden. We finished up the cheese and passed the jug of wine between us, draining it to the last drop.

"We can get water tomorrow at the stream," I said, wiping my mouth with the back of my hand. "We cross one before we reach the Thieves' Camp. And maybe, if we get lucky, we can kill some game."

Col looked at the crossbow that I had kept with me. "Do you know how to use that thing?"

"Of course," I lied. The crossbow was not really like my old bow. In theory, it worked in a similar way, but holding it felt... odd to me.

Col looked at me skeptically but didn't reply.

"How are you feeling?" I asked, to change the subject.

Col lifted his injured arm for the first time. "Still painful, but better. Though I still can't lift my sword." He showed me, trying to draw his sword with his right arm, with no results.

"And you can't use your left?"

"I can if necessary, but though my left arm is not weak, my right arm is always going to be better for battle."

"Hopefully, we won't have to battle anything before we get there."

He gave me a sharp look. "And when we get there?"

I shrugged. "We'll just have to wait and see."

"I thought you'd been there before."

"I have."

I tried to avoid the Thieves' Camp as much as possible. The people there—mostly men and a few hard women—never let a stranger go without some sort of cost. Whether they took it out of your flesh or your purse, you didn't just walk in and out for business without paying a price.

But there was no need to tell Col that, not yet. He needed to concentrate on getting better, and I didn't want to tell him until I had a plan.

We took turns sleeping, and Col insisted on the first watch. "Because you've been my guide all day," was all he said.

Gratefully, I sank against the hard stone, half sitting up. My entire body was feeling the effects of so much traveling and worry. Briefly, Flint's face drifted into my mind, but I stared into the fire to burn it out. There would be time for mourning him later, though I figured I'd never be over my grief. At least I'd been able to cover his body.

"What are you thinking about?" Col asked. "You're glaring at the fire."

"Nothing." I wrapped my new cloak around my shoulders and closed my eyes.

"Your friend..."

My eyes snapped open, and I silently dared Col to say anything about Flint.

He took the hint, and only nodded. "Goodnight, Samara."

At some point, I fell into a deep sleep, and my weariness was so complete that I didn't dream anything. Col woke me late into the night, and I knew he let me sleep too long. I chastised him for it as he laid his head back against the stone.

"You deserved it," was all he said. "And I'm feeling much better."

He fell asleep immediately, the slumber of a person who was used to sleeping out in the wild and had no trouble falling asleep on stony ground. I watched him for a while, followed his even breathing, which was a far cry from the death rattle of the day before.

This man was tough. I had seen plenty of people savaged by monsters, but never anyone who bounced back as quickly, and with wounds this grievous, his healing was even more remarkable.

"Where did you come from?" I whispered to myself. My stranger in black was mysterious. There were lines around his eyes, even though he had a young face. His armor was finely wrought, but had seen a great deal of use. I guessed him to only be a few years older than me, and yet, like me, I felt that he had seen a great deal in his life.

He was a survivor. I knew because one survivor always knows another.

However, at the rate he was healing, we could go our separate ways soon. Then we'd be square. He'd saved my life, I had saved his, and there would be no reason to keep traveling together.

The next morning, Col drank his tea before the sun was up, and we broke camp as soon as he was able. When we found a stream, I smirked.

"This is the stream you were looking for yesterday?" he asked skeptically.

"Yeah." Actually, we were significantly farther north than I'd thought we needed to be, and the stream here was narrower. But the landscape looked familiar again, and that was what counted.

Col stared at me, as if that was going to make me tell the truth. Instead, I sniffed and turned toward the crop of trees that had sprung up around the water. Col followed, shaking his head and muttering.

We continued for two more days, eating from our

dwindling supplies and talking little. Our pace improved every time Col drank the tea. But though his color was stable and he was steady on his feet, he could not grip anything with his right hand. I wondered if something important had been severed.

"Only time will tell," he said. "You've done wonders for me already, and now we can only hope that the tea does its work. If not, I shall have to learn to get by."

Once, we surprised a small goat grazing on the sparse grass of a hillside, and I raised my crossbow and fired off a shot. It went wide, striking the rocks above the goat and sending the animal running. The goat was gone before I could get another bolt loaded into the bow.

"Dammit."

"How good are you, really, with that thing?" Col asked when he'd stopped laughing.

Heat flushed my cheeks. "Not very," I admitted.

"Hm. It doesn't surprise me."

"And yet you believed my bluff when I had you as a target."

"I was delirious from monster venom and in significant pain, if you recall."

I grinned. "I'll never forget the way you just fell flat on your face. I'm surprised you didn't break your nose."

"And I'm surprised you don't know how to hunt, living in such an unforgiving land as this."

"There has never been much to hunt, but I'm not bad with a longbow. Mine was lost, however, when the soldiers..."

I didn't complete my sentence. Thinking about it only brought on a sense of panic. I often dreamed of that leering soldier with his hand down his trousers, and too often his face morphed into the mask of the Deviant. And the dream inevitably ended with Flint dying in gruesome ways.

Col didn't respond, and we walked on in silence.

On day five of our journey, we saw the Thieves' Camp at the base of a tall cliff, beneath the ruins of a long-abandoned castle on the mountain whose lone tower was bathed in clouds. The Thieves' Camp was well-hidden and well-guarded. We couldn't approach by the road, which meant we had a lot of climbing to do. And with dwindling food supplies making us ration, we were left with little breath for anything other than moving forward.

Finally, we stood atop a wooded ridge overlooking the camp. The scent of roast fowl drifted up from the cooking fires, and my stomach rumbled, but all I could see were the thatched roofs and the cliff face behind it.

I plunged into the trees to get a closer look, but kept an eye out for guards. As we approached, their absence became ominous. Finally, I came to a drop and got my first close-up look at the camp.

"Fuck," I said as Col joined me in my hiding place.

"Fuck," he agreed.

The Harrow's men were already there.

CHAPTER EIGHT

They had razed the camp, and several people were on their knees, tied and with soldiers standing over them with swords. The rest of the people were dead. Bodies lay everywhere, some of them with spears or arrows still sticking out of their backs where they'd been shot as they fled.

"Sons of bitches," I breathed. "We could have walked right into that. I count at least twenty. Any bright ideas?" I muttered. They were after the alicorn horn. They had to be.

"Can you sing and put them all to sleep?"

"There are too many of them. I'm... The magic isn't powerful enough for that."

I shook my head. The Harrow's soldiers weren't known for their mercy, but to kill that many people just for information about one magical artifact...

"I could use more of that wine right now," I groaned, wishing it wasn't gone.

"Looking to improve your aim?"

"If you don't have any ideas, just say so." Below us, there were screams, and threats from the soldiers. "I want to see what's going on."

I crept over the ridge and began making my way down the slope to a large boulder that would hide me. For a moment, I was out in full view of anyone who looked my way, but luck was with me, and as I slid behind the first large boulder, I glanced up. Col was frowning, and I could see his lips move with a curse.

But we didn't have any other options, and I didn't want to wait until the soldiers killed everyone.

I crossed from boulder to boulder, going downhill, ever closer toward the soldiers. Threats were causing screams among the captives, and I cringed. I didn't want to know what they were doing to them, but I couldn't afford not to.

Finally, I was as close as I dared, hiding behind the last place that would provide some shelter.

Snatches of conversation drifted over to me.

"Forfeit your eyes..."

I didn't hear the rest of it, but I knew enough about The Harrow's soldiers to know they were threatening to put out a man's eyes. And I knew enough to know they wouldn't hesitate to carry out the threat if it got them the information they wanted. There was a horrible shriek, and I recoiled, pressing myself into the rock.

"Prismvale," someone said. I didn't recognize the place, if that's what it was. Were they saying the thieves had gone to Prismvale, or that the captive was from Prismvale, or was he just screaming nonsense?

There were more demands, more screaming, but none of them brought any more information.

After listening for some moments, and after trying desperately not to imagine what was happening to the captives, silence fell. A man laughed, then there was the sound of a gauntleted fist striking flesh.

"No!" a man yelled. "I'll tell you!"

There was more muttering and curses. I couldn't hear, dammit. I crept around the edge of the boulders, peeking out enough to see who was speaking. It was an older man, or at least he looked older, but may have been my age. Times were hard, and young folks lived their whole lives in the span of twenty years. One of the soldiers grabbed the front of his shirt and dragged him through the blood-soaked ground away from everyone else, away from my hiding place.

For several tense minutes, everyone stayed as they were. Captives on their knees, their hands tied behind their backs, some of them bleeding profusely. One of them was pale and could barely stay upright, but every time he slumped toward the ground, a soldier grabbed his hair to jerk him upright.

There was another scream, and then the first soldier, who I guessed was the captain, returned without his captive, wiping blood off his sword.

"We ride," he shouted, "but first, cleanse this filthy den of thieves. Henrik, make the proper sacrifices. In the name of The Harrow!"

I knew what came next. I ducked behind the boulder and covered my ears. Despite every attempt to block it out, I still heard the soldiers killing off the remaining survivors, and their screams.

Instead of waiting there for someone to come around and find me, I retraced my steps and hid behind the first boulder near the ridge. Col was looking down at the carnage with a grim expression, but I didn't dare look back. I didn't need any more fuel for my nightmares.

Finally, I was relieved at the sounds of horses being ridden hard away from the camp, and when they faded, Col slid over the top of the ridge and came down to me, carrying our supplies.

"They killed them all," I said, trying to keep the shaking out of my voice. "Any chance of finding out about the alicorn horn is gone."

"It doesn't mean we can't still learn something," he said, and began to slide down the hill. In my heart, I knew he was right, but I didn't want to go. I hesitated, working up the courage to follow.

This journey had been pointless. All I wanted was to go home. But then I realized I had learned something. The captain had used the name "Henrik." Likely, these soldiers were the ones who had been hunting us, but they had found the Thieves' Camp instead.

And that meant they were no longer after me. Relief bloomed in my chest, and I gathered the courage to go after Col. I might be able to go home, but not without supplies.

I tried to avert my gaze from the corpses of beheaded men and gutted women, but Col was already searching the bodies. I began to take it seriously and search too. Always hungry, I munched on a dry crust of bread as I searched, though it was a gruesome process. Close to fifty people in all, and I shook my head. The Harrow's troops became more vicious and brutal with every passing year. The Harrow had won numerous battles, oppressed countless peoples, but he never seemed sated. And his thirst for blood spilled over into his soldiers.

Finally, Col and I met in the middle of the camp, and he frowned at me. "You could have been caught. And you would not have gotten a swift, clean death." He nudged the body at his feet, one that was missing its eyes.

"Worried about me?" I snipped.

"A misplaced concern, it seems. You're going to throw yourself into harm's way every chance you get."

"I don't like standing around talking, and there wasn't time to form a better plan, so I improvised," I said. "Anyway, let's get out of here."

Col gestured halfheartedly at the bodies. "I have heard tales of corpses who aren't buried becoming other things—monsters, apparitions, beasts that are doomed to wander."

"I've not only heard the stories, but I've seen it happen," I whispered. A body that was left for carrion didn't always just rot on the ground. I shuddered, remembering the dead villagers from the past winter.

"We could burn them," Col said. "And though I have no doubt that these people were not pure of heart, the world could use fewer monsters. However, it would take all day, and we don't have time."

"What does 'pure of heart' even mean?"

"A worthy discussion for another time." Col sighed.

"Every minute we delay is a minute the soldiers will be ahead of us. Did you hear any information we can use?"

"I only heard the name Prismvale, and I don't know where that is."

Col nodded. "I know and have been there, but it's leagues away, several days' ride from here. However, if the soldiers are headed in that direction, that's where we need to go."

"You want to follow the soldiers?" I asked incredulously.

Col nodded. "Follow them, and grab one to find out what he knows."

I gaped at him, wondering how in all the kingdoms were we going to manage that feat.

Col went over to some of the horses that hadn't been scared off and began checking them, lifting their feet and running his hands along their legs.

"What are you doing?" I asked with a sinking feeling.

"It's a sign of how rushed the soldiers were that they didn't take these mounts with them. Several of these horses are sound. If we ride, we have a hope of catching up to the soldiers. How else did you think we'd get to Prismvale?"

Col patted the neck of a brown horse and spoke in its ear. The horse tossed its head but then nuzzled his shoulder.

"There's only one problem with that idea," I said, remaining where I was, rooted to the ground and ignoring the stench of death around me.

"Just the one?" he asked as he led the horse away from the others.

"Yes, and it's a big one. I can't ride."

"You weren't afraid of the soldiers. Why a horse?" Col asked.

"Why am I afraid of the four-legged deathtrap? Anyway, I'm terrified of the soldiers, like any sane woman would be, but horses don't like me, and it's hard to go anywhere on one when it's in an enchanted sleep."

Col had left the brown horse and was untying another. My heart leaped into my throat.

"Anyway," I blurted, thinking of my family at home, and of Rose, who was probably sick with worry. "I can teach you how to make that tea. You've seen me do it enough times."

Col led the second horse toward me.

"Didn't you hear me? I'm not riding a horse."

I noticed he had done all his inspecting and leading with just his left hand, and I felt guilty. If he tried to fight, or capture a soldier, he was as good as dead.

"Will you go with me?" he asked, as if he'd been thinking the same. "This horse is calm enough to take a green rider."

I snorted. I'd never met a horse that would let me get near it, even if I'd wanted to.

"I still can't use my right arm," Col continued, "but I know where we're going. I'll be the guide, and you can be my right hand."

I laughed as an inappropriate joke leaped to my mind. I was so tired I was delirious. "Why would I travel any farther with you?"

"Because I can't wait until my shoulder heals to go after them, or the alicorn horn will be lost forever.

Those soldiers rode out of here like The Harrow himself was whipping them. They got the information they needed."

"Or they got the horn already."

"I don't believe so. Call it a gut feeling, but they are still after the true thief. There still may be a chance to stop them."

If I was honest with myself, finding that alicorn horn before those filthy soldiers did would feel good. It would be some vindication for everything that had happened.

And if we found the horn, I could steal it for myself. I could take it home to Laney, to make our lives normal. But now, I needed Col to find it. I didn't know where Prismvale was, nor how to keep up with the soldiers without being caught.

"Please," Col said. The pained expression on his face had me thinking that it wasn't a word he used often.

I sighed. "As soon as you're better, we go our separate ways. Agreed?"

He nodded. "Thank—"

I jabbed a finger at him. "If that four-legged beast bucks me off, you're on your own."

"It won't buck you off. And you'll be with me, no need to fear it."

"Don't tell me what to fear," I snapped. I began looking for supplies, trying hard not to think about riding a horse.

In my searching, I found the hilt to a sword half-buried in the mud, but when I uncovered it, I saw that the end had been broken.

"That one wouldn't have helped you anyway," Col

said from behind me. I hadn't even realized he was watching me.

"How about this one?" he asked. I turned to see him holding a short sword with a black hilt. "It's not as good as mine, but it's something. Are you better with a sword than you are with a crossbow?"

"No."

"Figured as much." He sheathed the sword and handed it to me. "You better be glad, siren, I was able to find you after you stole my sword."

His voice had taken on a threatening tone, and I almost laughed. Then I saw how serious he was. "Why?" I asked as he walked away. But he didn't answer. "Why, Col?"

He refused to answer the question and we continued searching the camp. We found quite a bit, as the soldiers had been worried about killing the people instead of looting the camp. There were dried meats and bread, cheeses, nuts, and even a few apples to pack into saddle-bags. Finally, I couldn't ignore it anymore when Col led one of the horses to me. "This girl is calm. You shouldn't have any trouble —"

The horse suddenly refused to move closer. She tossed her head, snorted, and began backing away.

"It's my siren blood," I said. "They know I'm different."

"Nonsense. They just sense your fear. Try to take a few calming breaths and relax, and I'll find a different horse."

But that horse spooked even harder, practically pulling Col off his feet before he could get it to calm down. I noticed how good he was with them, though, speaking to them softly until they stood still, snorting but no longer scared. They didn't fear him at all, and I'd never seen anything like it. I'd seen horses, of course, but never anyone who seemed to treat them as he did.

After the fifth horse spooked when it got close to me, he swore and glared at me. "None of the other horses would be good for a long journey. It has to be one of these."

"Do you think I'm trying to spook them? I'm just standing here."

He sighed. "There is another option. We load up that first horse with supplies, and you ride behind me on the other. Hopefully, it'll prevent both of you from being scared."

"*Right* behind you? As in, wrap my arms around you and snuggle you close?"

"For fuck's sake, woman. If we walk, we might as well go our separate ways. Because there's no way we're going to catch up with that company."

I sighed. "Okay. Let's try it."

He nodded and began speaking to the horse he had first tried to bring near me. "She's the biggest one and shouldn't have any trouble carrying us both." He spoke to her a few more moments, until she almost seemed to sleep. This man had a true gift with horses. It was like my ability, only for horses. When the mare was calm, he loaded the saddlebags onto the other horse and mounted the first.

Then he held out his left arm for me. Hesitantly,

trying not to let the horse know how terrified I was, I let him pull me up behind him.

I hadn't been this close to Col since I dragged him into the trees to treat his injuries. But now, instead of the foul stench of the monster's venom, I smelled man—sweat mixed with an earthy smell that reminded me of traveling through a forest in summer.

Man. All man.

The horse seemed to take me without any protests, and I knew that was only because Col was sitting with me.

Trying not to think about how close our bodies were, I hooked one arm around his waist for balance, and then took the reins of the second horse from him so he could guide ours.

"Grip the horse with your legs," he said. "Ready?"

I couldn't help noticing that his stomach muscles were rock hard, and even with his injury, Col's entire body carried an easy power. And I remembered how he had killed all those soldiers on his own.

I swallowed, hard. "Ready," I said, even if I wasn't.

CHAPTER NINE

"*T*his is the worst way to travel," I moaned sometime later. "My ass is already numb, and my thighs are turning gooey. Are you sure I'm supposed to grip the horse with them?"

"It works for everybody else," Col said. "It'll work for you, too. You just need some experience."

"Not an experience I've ever wanted," I muttered.

The first time we stopped to walk the horses, I almost fell to the ground—would have, if Col hadn't caught me with his good hand. I spent a few minutes rubbing my thighs and ass to get the blood back into them.

"It takes a bit of getting used to," he said.

"That's putting it mildly." Everything hurt. My ass, my thighs where they'd chaffed on the leather saddle, my arms from holding on to him so securely. It was a wonder he could still breathe, or that I hadn't cracked his ribs.

Walking worked out most of the kinks, but I was still sore, and by the time he hoisted me back onto the horse, I almost told him that the deal was off. But I wasn't a coward, and I paid my debts, at least those honestly taken on. So, I figured I'd toughen up.

The first night, we came to a stand of trees, and Col showed me how to tie the horses so they could graze without running off.

And then, too tired for anything else, I gratefully accepted the bread and cheese Col offered me and ate them quickly, washing them down with watered-down wine. I had finished my meager meal before Col had finished lighting the small fire.

"We're far away from the soldiers," he explained, "and you look frozen to that rock. Want more food?"

I nodded and reached eagerly for the food he offered me. While I scarfed down salty, tough meat, I caught him watching me. "What?" I asked around my large bite of food.

"Do you always eat like that?"

"Like what?"

"Like it's your last meal."

I swallowed the meat and tore off a big chunk of bread. "Is there any other way?"

He huffed a laugh but then got some food for himself, and ate much more slowly. Taking time to break the food into small bites and chewing each one carefully before swallowing. As if he had all the time in the world, and there would always be more. I imagined only rich people ate like that, though I had never seen one eat.

I looked at the hunk of cheese in my hand—the last thing I planned on eating before saving the rest—and shoved it all into my mouth. It was good. Sharp and soft and filling. I closed my eyes and moaned with the satisfaction of eating the whole thing and not having to share.

Col was looking at me with a raised eyebrow. I shrugged and finished off my wine.

"There's plenty here," he said seriously. "If you want more."

I shook my head. "We should save the rest for later. Who knows when we'll find more?"

He reached back into the bag and tossed me an apple. "We'll find more. Eat."

I ran my fingers over the bright red skin of the apple, something I hadn't eaten in ages. Finally, feeling guilty that I was eating meat, cheese, and apples when Laney might be going hungry this very minute, I bit into it with a satisfying crunch. It was sweet and juicy, and I polished it off in no time.

When I was done, I lay back with my hand on my belly, which was uncomfortably full. I wasn't used to eating so much in one sitting, and it was making small noises. To cover them up, I decided to make conversation.

"Will we catch them?" I asked. "The soldiers, I mean."

"We have to."

"Will you tell me why? Why are you after that alicorn horn, Col?"

Once again, he didn't respond, and I rolled my eyes at his secrecy. Fine, he could keep his secrets, and I would keep mine.

I dreamed for a few minutes of going home with the alicorn horn for myself. Of taking Laney and my father away from the bog and somewhere we could make a living. Without worrying about being hunted.

I could get rid of this monster inside of me, once and for all. And then I could make a life for all of us. I knew I could. We would find somewhere safe. Maybe I could take up hunting for real. I wasn't bad with a longbow—I hadn't lied about that. Just because there wasn't much to hunt didn't mean I didn't know how to kill it if there was. Or maybe I'd do something else, a trade of sorts. I was shit at sewing, but I was excellent at making brews and teas to help people. I could set up somewhere and help the sick. Didn't some people earn a living that way?

My thoughts continued to drift for a few more minutes, the noises in my stomach increasing all the while. Finally, a sharp burst of pain made me double over. It felt like some enormous creature was trying to burst out of my ass, and I clenched my butt cheeks together.

"What's the matter?" Col asked, his eyes full of concern.

"N—nothing," I said as my body suddenly went hot all over. I began looking around. I needed to... I needed some privacy. There were few trees, but plenty of rocks around. They would have to do.

Slowly, I stood. When that only intensified the pain in my belly, I jumped out of our little hollow and ran for a boulder a short distance away, yanking down my breeches and underthings and wincing at the cold air.

"Samara?" Col called from behind me.

"Don't follow me!" I yelled.

There were many things I wasn't shy about, but shitting myself in front of a stranger was one of them.

I didn't return to camp for almost an hour, and Col, seeming to know what was good for him, didn't comment on my absence or the reason for it. I only hoped he hadn't heard my audible and frequent sighs of relief as I paid the price for eating all that food in one sitting.

THE NEXT DAY, we found evidence that the soldiers had joined a large company. Col hoped that none of them had split off after that, or we would have a hard time figuring out who to follow. "The sooner we can sneak up on them and grab somebody, the better," he said irritably.

I felt helpless, knowing that my only value was in using my song to subdue an enemy. And I didn't discount that value, but it didn't stop me from feeling like dead weight most of the day.

However, whenever I gave Col his tea, I was reminded of why I was there and what was at stake. The movements in his right hand improved over the past few days, but he still couldn't do more than hold the reins.

"What's so special about your sword?" I asked him once. The weapon was still strapped to his back between the two of us. I looked at the gold hilt and bird carved into the center. "Would you really have hunted me down just for this?"

Col didn't reply, but there was no way he could have

missed the question. My mouth was literally right behind his ear.

The cold wind buffeted us, and I shivered, unconsciously shifting closer to Col's warmth. When he didn't protest, I waited for an answer.

"My father gave the sword to me," he said finally.

"Why? Were you rich?"

"Why do you ask that?"

"I just figured that anyone who has family heirlooms like a sword must have money to spare."

Col shook his head. "Those who know how to use a sword live and die by it. But that doesn't mean they have money. In fact, the sword may be the only thing of value that they have, but it keeps them alive."

"Like mercenaries."

He nodded. "And anyone else who values their life. Times are hard for everyone, Samara, not just in your little corner of the world."

I laughed. "I know. But I've never seen a sword as elegant as yours. Where did your father get it, and why did he give it to you?"

"My grandfather gave it to him, and my father gave it to me before he died."

"Oh," I said, shifting in my seat. "I feel like shit now."

"You didn't know."

"Either way, I'm sorry. My father is ailing, but I still have him."

"Your father?" he prompted.

"Yes. He is partly why you and I have crossed paths. If he weren't sick, I might be able to find work somewhere. As it is, I shouldn't leave him for long periods of time."

Yet here I am, riding farther away.

"Why can't you take him with you?"

I stayed quiet, unwilling to talk about Laney. Col didn't seem to care about my status as a half-breed, but the habit of keeping my sister a secret was too ingrained in me to let go of it now.

"He's part siren, too, or someone else is," Col guessed. "I should have realized that."

"It would be smart for me to go home now," I said, ignoring his guess. "But if there was one mage, there could be more, and anyone found with..." My cheeks heated and I was glad Col couldn't see them.

"Anyone found with you could be punished. That's what you were going to say, right?"

I nodded. "I could bring you trouble, too, though I'm guessing you can find it on your own."

Col laughed. "I can indeed."

"So, are you a mercenary?" I asked.

"Not quite," was all he would say.

After climbing gently rolling hills all day, we came to a flat plain that stretched out as far as the eye could see. In the distance was a large, dark, moving mass.

"That's our quarry," Col said, and picked up the pace.

"Won't they see us?"

"It's getting dark, and the setting sun will be in their eyes when they look this direction, so no."

We rode into the evening, finally slowing when Col thought we were within an acceptable distance. He didn't stop, however, and guessed the soldiers would push on until late into the night. It was a long, weary ride, and my butt was numb. My arms were stiff from holding on to Col for so long, and I kept fidgeting, trying to get comfortable. All I could think about was getting some sleep.

At one point, I dozed against his back, and my hand around his waist slipped low to rest between his thighs. I jerked awake and quickly adjusted my arm to the more neutral territory around his middle. I thought he huffed a laugh, but couldn't be sure.

"Tell me about your sword," I said to draw attention away from what I had just done. Col chuckled, and my face flushed at the obvious double meaning. "You know what I mean," I said determinedly. "Those are runes, right? Why do they glow?"

Col looked over his shoulder at me, a mischievous smile still lingering in his eye. "The sword's name is Bloodsong."

"You named your sword?" I asked. That was something I'd only heard of in stories.

"No. My great-great-grandfather did, and he had it crafted by some of the best blacksmiths to ever live—the dwarves. They imbued it with runes, and so with their own magic. That's why the runes glow in battle. It's been passed down from father to son ever since."

"The sword was never passed to a woman? Are you saying there are no women in your family, or that only men are allowed to have the sword?"

"It started as only men. My great-grandfather had an older sister, but she died. If she hadn't, the sword might have passed to her instead of him."

"How did she die? How do you know your great-grandfather didn't kill her?"

Col laughed. "She died in childbirth, or so I was told. I never knew either one of them, of course."

"Bloodsong.... The name makes me think it has seen lots of battles."

"It has," he said thoughtfully, "or so the song goes."

"There's a song?" I asked, sitting back a little to see his face, to see if he was making fun of me. "Who sings to their sword?"

"Songs have power, as you're well aware."

"Sure," I said. I wanted to laugh, but was proud of myself for keeping a straight face. "Well?"

"Well, what?"

"Aren't you going to sing for me? Tell me the history of this great sword!"

Col scoffed. "It would bore you to tears. You'd fall asleep and fall off the horse. Then what would I do with you?"

I rolled my eyes. "Probably toss me over the back of the other horse next to the saddlebags and keep going."

He chuckled quietly but didn't deny it.

I grinned. "You can't tell me there's a song about your sword, Col, and then do nothing for me."

Col was still laughing, but he finally nodded. "The tale starts with a stanza about the dwarven smith who forged the sword."

And then he began to sing, and I understood why he'd explained about the smith. The first part of the song was in another language, which I didn't understand. But then Col switched to the Common speech and sang of the sword once it was created, and things got more interesting. The first person to use the blade had killed five hundred men in one battle, and then named it Bloodsong. From there, each generation and each battle added to the song, and my companion sang late into the evening.

His singing voice was rough, but it was steady and soothing. If the story hadn't been so interesting, I would have fallen asleep like he predicted. But it held my attention, which seemed to make Col happy.

As we entered a grove of trees, Col finished his song, singing softly about the soldiers he had killed in the camp. He ended it on a sad note, and I stared at the back of his head for some time before saying anything. "That was beautiful," I said finally.

"I don't doubt that in your hands, Samara, it would be a thing of wonder, but I don't have your gift."

"I'll have to try and learn it, at least while we're on the road. Why are we stopping?"

"The horses need rest, and so do we. The soldiers will stop too, eventually."

We dismounted and began to set up camp a little way off the trail. There were signs everywhere of a large gathering of people and horses, leaving no doubt we were headed in the right direction.

"Will you teach me how to wield it?" I asked after we'd eaten a cold meal. It was too dangerous to light a fire now. Remembering my lesson about eating too much too quickly, I limited how much I ate and tried to mimic Col's method. Though I still finished long before he did.

"The sword?" Col asked. His gaze flicked to the sword belted at my waist. It had felt strange having it there, at least for the first few hours, but now it felt just as much part of me as his dagger.

"Do you know more about that sword than you do the crossbow?" he asked, amused.

"About the same," I admitted, "but I'm good with a knife. I'll show you with your own dagger."

"It's your dagger, now, and somehow, I believe you. I'll teach you how to fight with a sword, but you have to promise to do what I say. No sassy remarks."

I laughed now. "What about *saucy* remarks?"

Col smirked. "That's a whole other beast you might not want to deal with."

Heat ran through me, and I blinked. "Did you just make a joke?"

"Wouldn't you like to know?"

We sat there grinning at each other in the light of the moon. Finally, I shook my head. "I will... endeavor... to keep the snark out of my comments, if you will try not to be such an easy mark."

"Then maybe I will endeavor to teach you how to use that sword."

"I guess it's as close to a deal as we could wish for."

"Indeed."

CHAPTER TEN

A few minutes later, Col was laughing at the way I held my sword. "You're supposed to stab or slash your enemy, not bat them away like a fly."

"Look, I've seen people hold swords before. It's not that complicated."

"But like that, when you turn to deliver the blow, your sword is not going to hit its mark. It'll be the goat situation all over again."

I scowled.

"You've got to coax it, dance with it."

"Seduce it?" It was out of my mouth before I'd thought it through. My cheeks heated once again, but it was too dark for Col to see. Or so I hoped.

"Would you like to seduce my sword, Samara?" he said in a low voice.

This time, heat flushed other parts of my body, and I forgot what we were talking about. *Swords. Right.* "I thought you were supposed to do the seducing... when you sang to it."

Col laughed.

"Are you going to show me the right way to hold it or not?" I grumbled, getting irritated at the lack of progress and flustered at the way my body was betraying me. I was supposed to be learning, not flirting.

Wait, was it flirting? Goddess help me.

Col stopped laughing long enough to circle around behind me and put his hands on my hips.

I jerked away and faced him. "What are you doing?"

"Showing you how to stand. Come here." Col stepped in close, and I drew in a surprised breath. It shouldn't have mattered. I'd had my chest pressed up against his back all day, my legs straddling his backside, my arms around his waist.

While riding together was intimate in its own way, it was nothing compared to his gaze right now. He wasn't even touching me anymore. The moon gave off just enough light that I could see his mood had changed. The playfulness had fallen away. Now, he looked... intense.

My cheeks burned and no matter how much I wanted them to stop, they wouldn't. I held my breath, and just when I was starting to feel comfortable with his gaze, he broke the eye contact and positioned himself behind me again.

This time, I didn't stop Col when he put his hands on my hips. He rotated them until my left foot was slightly in front of my right, and then slid one leg between mine, nudging my feet apart. His touch was as light as a feather, and just like a feather, it sent shivers up my body.

"Like this," he whispered into my ear.

I bit my lip as he positioned my shoulders. His left

hand was warm and strong, and though I could tell his right hand was still weak, it felt heavy and comforting on my shoulder.

I almost protested when he broke contact, putting enough distance between us to circle me, correcting my position where it was needed, and having me hold out my sword arm while he corrected my grip.

"For a person of my size, this would not be a two-handed sword," he said, "but you are smaller, so I'm going to show you how to wield it with both hands. The pommel can support your left hand, like this." He had me grip the pommel, or the very end of the hilt. "Use your left hand to swivel, and your right hand to grasp it. And don't forget to coax it, to caress it. If you try to bully it into moving, it'll be work, and you'll never master it. But if you enjoy the experience, the world opens at your feet. Don't force anything."

I snorted. "You sound like a man talking to a lover instead of a sword."

Col grinned. "It is much the same. Although," he said, leaning in close to whisper in my ear, "my lovers *always* enjoy the experience."

I stood there, dumbfounded, as he raised his own sword. *Pay attention, Samara.*

Col pretended like he hadn't just stepped beyond innuendo and into the danger zone, and began showing me the moves, which were mostly about moving my feet and the sword to follow. Each time, he placed his hands on me to show me exactly where to stand. Each time, I didn't protest.

Finally, after showing me a couple of moves and

making me copy them without help, he declared an end to the lesson and went back to sit down against the pack he was using as a pillow.

"Remember the steps for tomorrow," was all he said. And then he lay back and was immediately asleep.

I sheathed my sword and sat down with a huff. "Guess I'm keeping first watch," I said to myself.

Wide awake, and with a heat on my skin that had nothing to do with the mild exertion, I watched him far into the night.

THE NEXT DAY, we caught our first glimpse of the soldiers since we'd left the mountains.

Col dropped back. "If we can see them, they can see us. We'll close more distance between us at nightfall."

"And you're really going to try to catch one of them?"

"Not just me," he stated matter-of-factly. "You are an integral part of my plan. Unless you're afraid?"

"What's to be afraid of? Only more soldiers than we can count, armed to the teeth and with blood on their minds. Against the two of us—an injured warrior and a half-breed siren. Though I suppose now that you've taught me those moves, I can fight anybody."

"I would like to see that."

"See me get killed, you mean? Because my songs are not powerful enough to subdue that many at once."

Col glanced at me. "Why do you call yourself that word?"

"What, a half-breed?" I shrugged.

"An ugly term. Words have power, Samara."

"I know that," I said, irritated.

"And yet you denigrate yourself with that label, as if you believe you are less than others."

I didn't respond. In the eyes of the law and most of the people I'd met, I *was* less than them. "Why do you care?"

Col halted the horses and looked back at me over his shoulder. "Because it doesn't matter what your ancestry is, but rather what you do with it. Monsters take many forms, but it has nothing to do with the blood in their veins, and everything to do the condition of their heart." He spoke firmly, resolutely, and I wondered if we were still talking about the same thing. "There are all sorts of monsters in the world, Samara, but you are not one of them. Don't let anyone tell you any different."

"What would you call me, then?"

Col smirked. "By your name, of course. But also... A songbird, maybe. My little songbird. Or my little siren. I'll have to figure out which one you are."

Heat traveled through my body, and I hoped Col didn't notice the hitch in my breathing. "Good luck with that." I smiled, and he laughed.

We dismounted and walked. It was a relief to see our targets in the distance, but they also filled me with dread.

"Exactly what is the limit of your power?" he asked after a moment. "For future reference."

"It depends on the people," I answered. "If they are strong-willed, then twelve at the most. But if they are weak, fifteen to twenty, depending."

"Depending on?"

"On how I'm feeling that day," I said exasperatedly. I was leading the pack horse, who, while obviously not wanting to come close to me, resorted to simply tossing his head in protest.

"Have you always had your gift?"

"Yeah." I shrugged. "As long as I can remember. My father said it started about the time I began talking. And then, when I found out what I could do... well, let's just say I was hell as a three-year-old."

"Still are."

I narrowed my eyes at Col but let it slide. He said nothing else, as if hoping I would say more. Somehow, I felt easy around him now, and the words spilled out of me of their own accord.

"For a long time, my parents didn't tell me what I was; they only begged me to stay silent about my ability. In a time when witches and half-breeds were being hunted down and tortured, they alternated between scolding and cajoling me for wielding my gift of song. Anything to keep me from revealing my true ancestry. And I didn't know why. My parents looked perfectly normal.

"Then my brother came along, and anyone who looked at him could tell he wasn't fully human. Finally, my parents explained that I was part siren, and I realized what I was.

"A despised half-breed.

"My parents had left our village after my brother was born, seeking to move to a better place just as The

Harrow began spreading his hate and conquering lands beyond his own borders.

"We lived in poverty for years, moving whenever my parents feared discovery. By then, Flint moved with us too. My parents didn't have much, but they couldn't leave an orphan on the road to starve, even when so many others said it was better for him to die than live with his disability. In The Harrow's world, all aberrances were feared and reviled.

"A few years later, Laney was born, and then the unthinkable happened—a roving band of runaway soldiers found us. Deserters, but that didn't mean they were any less forgiving. They raided our poor village, and, taking one look at my brother, slew him where he stood.

"My mother tried to stop them, and they attacked her, too," I finished. "Beat her, abused her. She only lived a few days after that."

From there, my father and I had survived on hate alone, hate for the soldiers who had taken his wife and son from him, my mother and brother from me, hate for the emperors and kings who played with our lives.

Col silently walked beside me for a long while after I finished. Finally, he said, "I lost my parents, too." He twisted one of the rings on his left hand, the ruby one encircled with gold branches. "This was my mother's."

"I'm... sorry," I said. "How did they die?"

"They were murdered," he answered quietly.

I waited for him to elaborate, but he didn't. Embarrassed that I had shared so much of my personal history with him, without it being reciprocated, I didn't speak as we made camp in the dark. Asshole, I thought. But it made me more curious about him than ever.

I wanted Col to teach me more about swordplay, and even dared to wonder how it would feel to have his hands on me again. But the air between us had grown suddenly strained, and I couldn't bring myself to ask.

It was just as well. I had already revealed too much about myself, but it didn't have to become more than that. I'd spent the previous night thinking while I was on watch, and had concluded that the flirting was acceptable, but I couldn't let myself fall for this guy. He was obviously high born, and therefore not for me, but that wasn't the biggest hurdle. I planned to steal that alicorn horn for myself, if I ever got the chance, and couldn't afford any distractions or entanglements.

Col offered to take the first watch, so I jumped at the opportunity for sleep.

As planned, we woke in the wee hours of the morning, leading our horses toward the soldiers' camp, over the churned ground. As soon as we were close enough, Col handed me his horse's reins and crept ahead. He was so quiet he could have been a ghost or apparition moving over the dry grass, and soon he was lost to my sight.

I waited silently, moving little so I didn't scare the horses. I'd learned that though they disliked my presence, they liked the sound of my voice even less.

For several tense moments, all I could do was stare into the darkness and wait.

"Samara," said a voice sometime later, whispered almost as if it were on the wind. Then Col materialized from the grass beside me, and I nearly jumped out of my skin.

The horses, grazing now, didn't even flick an ear.

"Not tonight," was all he said. Then he took the reins and led us away from the soldiers' camp.

"Why not tonight?" I asked when we were safely out of earshot and the campfires were mere pinpricks on the horizon.

"Because right now they're on high alert, and I don't know if it's because they spotted us today, or some other threat is looming. We'll take a wait-and-see approach."

We waited in the dark. There was nothing else to say, and I was tired. Periodically, I dozed, startling myself awake many times as the night grew colder. Snow flurries drifted around us, and I longed for a campfire, but it was too risky. Once again, my thin cloak would have to do.

"They certainly don't mind everyone seeing where they are," I said.

"Yes, and that concerns me. We are technically on The Harrow's conquered lands, but there's always a possibility of raiding parties from Glimmerdale."

Glimmerdale was the elven kingdom to the far west, on the other side of the Fell Marshes, which ran north to south for many leagues. I only lived in the small southern portion. "Why would Glimmerdale be this far into Harrowfell?" I asked. "Are they at war with The Harrow too?"

Col's voice grew hard. "Everyone is at war with The Harrow, but there are few left to stand up to him these days. Though some haven't given up hope."

"Maybe the soldiers think there are too many of them to be bothered."

"Then they would be arrogant indeed. The Harrow has grown fat on his success, and his generals are too busy with wine and women to maintain order. I don't like the feeling in the air," he said. "We'll see what happens before morning."

I had lived my life surrounded by battle and war and starvation, though I didn't know what Col was talking about. He sensed something that I didn't understand, but I had no reason to doubt his instincts.

Neither of us slept the rest of the evening, watching the distant fires while the horses grazed.

Just before dawn, the sound of a horn sang over the plain. Col was already watching, and I joined him. The fires in the distance flickered and then changed, spreading in the dry grass. Even from here, we heard shouts and the ring of steel on steel.

"The company has been attacked," he said. "I think now might be our best chance to get some information."

"In the middle of a battle?"

"It'll be a great distraction. No one will be paying attention to us."

We readied the horses and then waited for dawn to show us what was happening. The day dawned golden, except for where the battle raged on.

Sunlight glinted off steel. A large band was harrying the company, their archers and swordsmen having already broken through the ranks. And the fire was indeed spreading over the plain, burning up the dry grass and blowing to the east.

I also saw that we had journeyed to the end of the plain overnight, with new mountains within sight to the north.

"Leave the pack horse," Col said. "We'll come back for it."

Col slung himself into the saddle and helped me up behind him. I'd barely got my arms around his waist before we took off straight for the battle. The smoke hung in the air, making it harder to see what was happening, and with a growing stab of anxiety, I tried to peer around Col. All I managed were a few glimpses before he pushed me back behind him.

It was a desperate fight. Bodies already littered the ground, and the screams of the dying mingled with the other sounds of battle to form one discordant shriek, as if the plain itself was protesting the carnage.

"Look," Col said, turning the horse. "Some of Harrowfell's soldiers are deserting."

He was right—a couple of soldiers had broken off from the battle and were riding away.

"That's our chance," he said, and then he urged our horse into a canter, trying to intercept the nearest deserter.

But the soldier's horse was bolting, spurred on by fear and running half-wild. As we tried to cut them off, the rider saw us and managed to turn his mount away, toward the foothills. And then we were in an all-out chase and losing ground.

"We're too slow!" I yelled. "Get off."

"Excuse me?" Col asked.

"Get off the horse, Col!"

He halted the horse and slid onto the ground in the same movement. I scooted forward in the saddle, and tried to put my feet into the stirrups. They were too long for me, having been adjusted for Col's long legs. There was no time to change them. Every second counted, so I did what he had told me and gripped the horse with my legs. Then, without giving the mare a chance to think about the fact that I was her new rider, Col gave her a pat on the hindquarters and sent her leaping forward. My breath was taken away by the horse's speed and I held on for all I was worth.

With her burden considerably lighter, the mare ran flat out. Her ears were pinned to the back of her head, and I didn't know what that meant, but I concentrated on using my legs to keep my seat and watching the ground close between us and the deserter. He looked back a few times, but instead of veering away, only tried to go faster. I slipped into the rhythm of the mare's stride, and for the first time thought I understood why people liked horses. She practically glided over the grass. It was like flying.

The deserter's horse couldn't outrun mine, and when the soldier saw he couldn't escape, he wheeled his horse and drew his sword.

But I wasn't about to get close enough to let him stab me.

Reining in my mare like I'd seen Col do, I brought her to a halt. She tossed her head and half reared, and I held on for dear life. But I had enough presence of mind to remember what I was supposed to be doing, and began to sing, directing my magic toward the deserter.

He didn't even know what hit him. One minute, he

was raising his sword in warning, and the next, he was falling out of the saddle.

It happened so fast, my song hadn't had a chance to work on either horse. The soldier's mount bolted, dragging him over rough grass with his foot caught in the stirrup.

But then Col was there on our other horse, cutting off the spooked animal and grabbing its reins, speaking in that low, soothing voice of his.

It was too bad that the soldier hadn't been dragged just a little bit farther. I had no pity in my heart for him, no room for mercy.

But we needed him, so, still singing, I awkwardly got to the ground and allowed the mare to back away from me. The soldier's chest rose and fell in a deep sleep.

"All too easy," I said. "He is weak-minded."

"That was some good riding," Col said, and a surge of pride washed through me. "Perhaps I'll make a horsewoman out of you yet, Samara."

Then he was rolling the soldier over and stripping him of his weapons. It took the two of us to get him over the back of the packhorse, but I was glad to see that Col's arm, though still weak, had more function than it did the day before.

"At this rate, you soon won't need me around at all."

Col grunted noncommittally, caught our mare, and helped me back into the saddle.

"Are you walking?" I asked.

In answer, Col hopped up behind me.

His chest pressed against my back, and his arm around my waist was more comforting than I wanted to admit. My heart had been racing from the chase, and yet, just the feeling of Col nearby, breathing evenly and holding me tight, calmed me. I was... safe. Something snapped into place for me, and I realized I hadn't felt that way in a long time.

We rode the horses away from the battle as fast as we dared but not enough to overtax the horses again. Or to draw any attention to ourselves.

We left the soldier's horse to roam, as it had run off as soon as we let it go.

Periodically, I would turn in the saddle and sing to our captive to keep him sleeping, but by the time we reached the foothills, he was groaning softly, groggy but almost awake.

It was perfect timing.

Col jumped down and grabbed the soldier, who groaned as he flopped to the ground. He had blood on his cheek but otherwise looked unharmed.

When he saw us, he looked scared. Perhaps he sensed our grim determination because he recoiled and tried to crawl away. Col drew his sword and stepped on the man's back, placing his blade at his throat.

"Fuck!" said the soldier. "I done nothing. Let me go!"

Climbing out of the saddle, I hung back, waiting to see how this would unfold. Beyond capturing the man, I had no idea how we were going to get information out of him. With a chilling thought, I wondered what Col had in mind. I hadn't taken him for a torturer, but the look in his eyes was murderous.

"What is your name?" Col asked steadily. He kept his

blade at the man's throat, his foot on his back. The man had frozen, and I realized something.

Col had chosen to go after a deserter because this man would do anything to save his own skin. And if he knew any information at all, it might not be difficult to get it out of him.

"Your name, deserter," Col urged.

"Jorvan," he said in a trembling voice.

"Okay Jorvan, this is what's going to happen. I have some questions for you. If you answer them truthfully, you will live. If you lie or refuse to answer, I will begin cutting your body, and if you still refuse, I will take your head clean off your shoulders. Since you seem to value your life, I'm hoping you'll cooperate."

"Y—yeah—yes. I'll tell you anything. Though I don't know much, as I was conscripted. So no ransom will be coming for me."

"I don't care about ransom. What was your company's errand, before the attack this morning?"

"I... I don't rightly know. We were on our way to Prismvale, and in a hurry."

"And what were you going to do in Prismvale?"

"We were looking for somebody."

"A whole company for one person?"

"I suppose," the deserter said. "It was a thief. Please, please that's all I know."

A shudder ran down my spine, and I was relieved not to be their prey now. "Do you think he's lying?" I asked.

Col didn't move his sword. "No. I believe him."

I waited to see if Col would kill the man, almost wished for it. The thought made me sick, but only a little.

After what soldiers like him had done to my family, I had no pity for them. The anger that washed over me left a bitter taste in my mouth.

The deserter also seemed to be wondering about his fate. "Wh—what'll you do with me?"

"We will give you rest." Col nodded to me.

Swallowing my anger, I sang once again, directing the magic toward the deserter, and he immediately went back to sleep. Only when his breathing deepened did Col remove his foot and sword. Then he began to tie him up, binding his hands and his feet. He tossed the soldier's weapons into the grass nearby. The soldier would be able to free himself when he woke.

I watched all of it with a quiet fury.

"We can't kill him in cold blood, Samara," Col said softly. He had walked to my side, but I barely registered it, reviling the deserter for the evil thing he was. A man just like this had killed my brother and mother, had ripped them from me in a moment's time.

"You..." I choked out, "have no idea how much he doesn't deserve your mercy."

"This is not the man who killed your mother. We don't know why he's here. And because of that, we cannot pronounce judgment on him."

"Isn't it enough to know that he's in The Harrow's service?" I glared at Col now, staring up into his face and hating the look of pity there. "The Harrow's armies have done nothing for this land but bring misery. And if this soldier was with them, then he is one of them."

"But we don't know what he had to do to ensure his

own survival. No, something tells me letting him live is the right thing. I feel it in my gut."

He glanced down at my hand, which rested on the hilt of my dagger. It would be so easy to slip my blade between the soldier's shoulder blades. And then it would be done. One less scourge on the land.

Col met my eyes again, this time not with pity but with sorrow. "I know how it feels," he whispered. "Truly I do. Not that I have been through everything you have, but I know what it is to hate. Don't give in to it, Samara."

My jaw quivered as I stared into Col's eyes. "It's too late for me," I whispered.

He held my chin. "Then I ask you to trust me, in this at least. Let the man go."

"And if I don't?" I hissed in a flash of anger. "What would you do if I buried this dagger in his back? Would you stop me?"

It was a challenge, and the air between us practically crackled with the dare. Finally, Col dropped his hand and took a step back. "No, I will not stop you," he said. "This is your choice."

I swallowed, my mouth suddenly dry. With my dagger in hand, I stood over the bound, sleeping soldier.

Trust me, Col said. I realized that I did trust him, a little. But who was he to ask me not to do this thing? The Harrow had taken everything from me. I might not even be able to go home without risking Laney's life. I'd be doing the world a favor if I got rid of this soldier.

I readied myself, planting my feet, preparing to drive the tip of the dagger into the deserter's back. It would only take a second, and I wondered what it would feel like. Would I hear the blade slide through bone, or smell the blood right away? How long would it take him to die, and would he feel any pain as he slept?

I hesitated. The man was just sleeping, his face calm and seemingly without worry. I realized how young he was, no older than me. And a flash of red hair peeked out from under his helmet. He could have been Flint.

My heart broke anew. Flint had been killed as he ran, shot in the back before he knew what was happening to him.

Tears welled in my eyes, and I blinked furiously. Finally, I sheathed my dagger and stepped away from the soldier. Burning with feelings I could only describe as guilt and shame, I turned away from Col so he wouldn't see them on my face.

"Where do we go from here?" I asked.

CHAPTER ELEVEN

*W*e left the deserter behind, took our horses, and made for the foothills. Col knew the location of Prismvale, a small city on the edge of Harrowfell, controlled by its soldiers.

"How are we going to overtake the soldiers and get to the thief first?" I asked. The thief we *hoped* had the alicorn horn. It was the only lead we had, though, so it was either give up or follow the trail. "I suppose it's too much to hope that they were all killed," I muttered.

Just because I didn't want to kill one in cold blood didn't mean I couldn't wish for their deaths, right?

Trust me, Col had said. I was weary, resigned to letting him lead. For now.

I watched him unsaddle the horses, using both hands. Soon, he really wouldn't need me. Might not even need me now.

I took a deep breath. I had helped Col, and now he had a destination. Our debts were settled. For a moment, I considered parting ways, but I didn't know where Prismvale was, and to leave Col now would be giving up on the alicorn horn. And I couldn't, not yet.

The more I considered it, the more I figured it was the right course of action, a reason for being gone from home for so long. If I came back with a life-changing gift, it would all be worth it. To be rid of my cursed half-breed self... to rip it out of my body and start a new life sounded like a fairy tale come true.

"We'll leave the horses here," Col was saying. "I know a shortcut, a way to get to Prismvale before The Harrow's men. We'll go over the mountains while they go around. We might even be there days ahead of them. But it involves climbing, and it's no country for horses, even ones as good as these."

He whispered in the mare's ear, and she nuzzled his shoulder.

I swallowed a twinge of regret. Just when I was starting to like the horses. "Good riddance," I said, but without any conviction.

"The thing about you is," Col said as he gave the mare a final pat, "I can always tell when you're lying, Samara."

My ears burned with heat. The last few days, it had seemed like Col could look straight into my soul to know what I was thinking or feeling.

And yet, it hadn't scared him off. A point in his favor.

"So we just set them free," I said, daring to step closer to the mare. She shook her head when I came near but then went back to grazing. Acceptance, only now I didn't need it. I touched her neck and then gave it a soft pat. "If there are any gods up there to listen," I whispered, "I hope they'll give you a break. You're too nice a girl to have a hard life."

Then, picking up one of the saddlebags and gathering my pack, I followed Col on foot.

We didn't look back.

Almost immediately, we were picking our way over rocks and scree that threatened to twist an ankle if you put a foot down wrong. There were a few trees, but mostly it was bare rock and some brave shrubs.

By the end of the day, I was completely exhausted, but I didn't want to admit that to Col, so I kept following him, picking my way until it was so dark that we had to stop. In the distance and far below, the fire still burned unchecked on the grassland.

Once again, I was reminded of the waste of war.

We couldn't light a fire. Anyone who had survived the battle below, whether they were looking for runaways or not, would see it. Col hadn't drunk his tea since this morning, and without a fire, I couldn't brew more. I settled for making it with cold water, but the effect was greatly diminished.

"It's not just deserters and The Harrow's men we have to worry about," Col said, after he stopped making a face at the taste of the cold brew. "These mountains are notorious haunts of the worst kinds of monsters, human and beast. I will not risk a fire unless it's the only thing between us and freezing to death."

"That seems likely," I muttered, shivering. It was colder up here, and I brought my knees up to my chest and wrapped my cloak around my body try to keep warm. Not for the first time, I wished we had heavy blankets. Or that I wore woolen clothes.

Col unclasped his cloak and handed it to me. "Here. I'm not cold yet."

I threw it over my shoulders and shivered. Col's cloak was heavy and big enough to swallow me, and I reveled in the feeling of finally being warm. But then I caught him looking at me, and I changed my seat to sit beside Col. With a small smile, I wrapped one side of the cloak around him and the other around me, placing my shoulder next to his. "There's no reason we both can't use it," I said.

He didn't say anything but moved to wrap his arm around me beneath the cloak. It was warmer this way, and I wasn't about to protest. I'd already spent several days pressed up against him.

"Get some sleep, little siren," he said. "I'm afraid you're going to need it."

I was going to argue with him, to say I was stronger than he was and didn't need anyone to tell me what I needed. But my feet were bruised from the day of climbing, and my legs had burned coming up that last slope. Tentatively, I rested my head on his shoulder, and when he didn't protest, I tucked my arms around my body and fell into a fitful sleep plagued with nightmares.

STRONG ARMS WRAPPED AROUND ME, and I lashed out wildly. Fighting, yelling, kicking. There was a grunt, and then the arms released me. "Samara," came Col's pained voice.

I sat up, sweating, my heart hammering. There was no fire to see by, nothing but the moon giving off weak light overhead. The sweat on my skin quickly made me shiver, and I reached for the cloak tangled around my legs. I realized where I was, who I was with.

Col was crumpled nearby, cursing under his breath. "What happened?" I asked, pulling my thin cloak around me.

"You had a nightmare," he said, easing up into a sitting position. His voice still sounded weak. "I tried to wake you."

I remembered parts of it now. The Harrow's soldiers had been taking their turns with me while the Deviant had watched, his robes hiking up near his knees and...

I took a deep, steadying breath. The nightmare had been worse than what had actually happened. But I still couldn't get rid of the dirty feeling left behind, like tiny bugs crawling beneath my skin. I shuddered. "You tried to wake me?"

"You were thrashing and calling out, and when I tried to help, you kicked me," he said accusingly.

I didn't need to ask where I had kicked him. Must have been an instinct, even in my dreams, and I tried not to smile. "Sorry," I said. "Are you all right?"

Col shook his head. "Your kick was perfectly targeted. What about you?"

"I'm fine."

"You didn't sound fine."

"It was just a dream," I snapped. I didn't want to

relive it, nor did I want to talk about it. We sat in silence a few moments. Finally, I stood and pulled the cloak in tight around me. "You can sleep. I'll keep watch."

Col watched me pace back and forth a bit before lying down with his own heavy cloak. I longed for more heat, any heat, but I didn't dare ask if I could snuggle up to him again. He was getting too familiar, and I had been letting my guard down. I paced and watched, trying to get the nightmare out of my head but not succeeding.

After a few minutes, I knew he wasn't sleeping. He was too busy trying to keep an eye on me.

"What?" I asked.

Col stood and tossed his cloak over his shoulder. Then he drew his sword with his right arm, which was still weak. "How about some practice?"

"Now?" I asked.

"You got something better to do?"

I shivered again. At least moving around would warm me up. I drew my sword. It still felt awkward in my hands, but I remembered Col's earlier lesson and adjusted my grip. Tonight, there were no hands on my hips to correct my stance. He wanted me to remember and do it for myself.

"Drop your shoulders and straighten your spine," he commanded, and I found myself doing as he said. My mind relished the idea of giving into his orders, relieved from having to think about the horrors of my nightmare. "Relax."

I scoffed. "How do you relax when you're pointing a sword at someone?"

"You relax because you know that blade is standing

between you and them. That it won't let anything through... if that's what you wish."

"Easy enough for you to say," I muttered.

Col smirked. "With experience comes confidence. Now, give me your best attack."

"You want me to attack you?"

"I want you to try. But not with your knee this time—your sword."

I smiled. Taking a deep breath, I lunged for Col. Our swords connected as he parried. Even with his bad arm, he moved his sword once and sent me sliding away from him. I felt a sharp smack on my backside, and yelped.

"What the hell?" I asked, spinning around.

Col showed me the flat of his sword and grinned. "That was terrible. Try again."

Rubbing my ass to take the sting out, I sent a few muttered curses in his direction.

"Quit stalling," he said, standing with his longsword loose at his side.

Without warning, I raised my sword and lunged again, this time aiming lower. Again, he sent me spinning around with another sharp smack on my ass.

"Cut it out!" I yelled, growing angry.

"Make me," he said.

I tried. Gods, I tried. Over and over again, Col evaded or parried my attacks with seemingly no effort. And each time I missed him, he smacked my ass with the flat of his sword. Not enough to do any damage, but enough to sting, and I began cursing him with every heaving breath. I wanted to rage at him for his arrogance, to hack his body into little bits and scatter them to the wind. Just then, I hated him more than I had hated anybody.

My attacks grew more frenzied and less effective, and I yelled as my frustration grew.

"You're not trying hard enough, Samara."

"Asshole!" I yelled as I gulped in air.

The next time, with one small motion, he sent me reeling toward the sharp rocks behind us. But I was more worried about his sword on my ass than those rocks, and instead of letting my momentum carry me forward, I managed to sidestep and pivot.

My sword clanged with his, which had been on its way to making another red mark in my flesh.

Surprised at my success, I lost my footing and almost fell. When I recovered, Col was standing in front of me with his sword at my throat. I had expected a compliment, but that's not what came out of his mouth.

"You are too slow, siren. I could have killed you. Next time—"

"Next time turn your back to me and see how my sword feels on *your* ass," I hissed. Maybe I would shove it up his ass and be done with him.

He lowered his sword and smirked. "I'd rather not lose it completely."

"Maybe that's my intention," I snarled.

"Next time," he continued, completely unruffled, "press your advantage. You don't have the luxury of falling. If you fall, you're dead."

I darted for him, enraged at his calm voice, at his lack of compassion. This time, with one move from him, my sword went spinning out of my hand. I yelled and attacked again, moving inside his reach and attempting to drive my shoulder into his stomach. He stepped aside, and this time I did slam into the rocks, flat on my face.

My still-sore jaw erupted in new agony, and I tasted fresh blood. And, to add insult to my injuries, there was another sharp *smack* on my backside, even while I lay face down on the cold ground.

Col turned me over with his foot, and I groaned.

"Congratulations," he drawled, "you just got yourself killed."

"I HATE YOU," I said, massaging my sore ass as I walked. We had broken camp at dawn and were climbing ever upward, and I had cursed Col at every step.

"So you keep saying," he said from above. "How's your jaw?"

"Why do you care?" I spat back. It was swollen, and I had cut my chin on the rocks. But there would not be any other lingering damage, provided I didn't keep injuring it.

The "lesson" had ended after my fall. Breathing hard and in pain, I had sat gingerly away from him the rest of the night, too angry and sore to speak to him.

Col's shortcut was worse than the road. We had crested the first steep ridge only to see another, higher one in front of us. Cursing under my breath, I followed Col down, which was just as dangerous, if not more so, than going up. More than once, I landed on my butt when rocks moved beneath my feet. Each fall reminded me of my failure of the night before, and each twinge of discomfort reminded me of my seething anger at Col and the flat of his blade.

Eventually, hiking up the next ridge became more of a climb, and we had to pull ourselves up on ledges so we could continue walking.

"It's a shortcut, he says," I grumbled.

Col laughed. "All roads have a cost, especially shortcuts."

"No doubt a wisdom gained from getting lost all the time."

"No. Wisdom from my father. But I have always found it to be true," he said with a smile. It lit up his face like sunlight on a cool autumn morning. He had been in a particularly cheerful mood all morning, which I could only guess was a result of my humiliation during the night.

"My father was a bit more practical," I said, "like don't go looking for trouble when there's plenty standing next to you." I put as much venom into the words as I could, and Col paused to look at me.

"It sounds like you listened to your father about as much as I listened to mine."

I scowled.

"Would you like me to massage your ass for you?" he asked matter-of-factly.

I took a step away from him. "Don't touch me."

He nodded. "You're angry."

"And you are a pig." I stood up straight, glaring into his eyes. "And an asshole."

Col shrugged. "Perhaps, but nothing is fair when it comes to fighting for your life."

"You were supposed to be teaching me, not beating my ass like you have some sort of kink."

He grinned then. "That's the second time you've asked about my kinks—"

"I didn't ask about them!"

"You like to fantasize, though, which makes me wonder what yours are."

I picked up a rock and threw it at his head. He ducked and laughed. Finally, he sighed. "You may not approve of my methods, but you'll never forget to watch your backside when you're in a fight. And..."

I crossed my arms over my chest. "And what?" I asked impatiently.

"You forgot your nightmare," he said seriously.

Dammit, he was right. The effort and the pain of my "lesson" had driven those images straight out of my head. This morning, they were mostly foggy remnants that lacked any real threat.

"You're still an asshole," I said. "And if you ever touch my ass with any appendage again, I'll put you to sleep and cut it off. And if it's your precious Bloodsong, I'll use the flat of it to beat you bloody."

Col inclined his head, as if he figured I just might follow through on that threat, and we continued our climb.

I used my anger as fuel and threw myself into the journey. Part of the way up we ran into a wall, which was going to require real climbing, actual mountain climbing that meant placing our feet just right so we didn't fall to a terrible death below. Anger, I could use, had learned to live with. But I had to keep moving forward.

Out of my element, I followed Col, placing my hands where he placed his, doing the same with my feet.

Watching him so closely, I noticed his right arm was giving him trouble, and how careful he was not to put all his weight on it. At one point, it gave out completely, and he almost fell and took me with him.

Served him right for using it last night. He must have injured it again during our "lesson." And I hadn't been able to properly brew the tea for over a day now.

After Col had steadied himself, I moved to the side and began finding my own handholds. If he fell, I didn't want to go with him.

At this point, my fingers were bleeding. Even the calluses couldn't protect them against this rock that sought to destroy my body. But all I thought about was the next handhold–not of slipping and falling to my death. I moved one limb only when the others were in place, keeping an eye on Col the whole time.

Slowly, we made progress. It was rough going, but I felt a great rush when my hands found the top. *Careful don't celebrate yet.* I crawled over onto what was a deep, comfortable ledge and removed my pack and saddlebag. It was amazing they had made it this far. I had been certain the supplies would have been dumped by now.

Positioning my body so I could lean over the edge safely, I watched Col struggle the last few feet.

"You're almost there," I called down. "Let me help you. That arm could give out at any moment."

"I'm all right, siren."

"I don't want to scrape your body off the rocks below. And if I have to find my way out of here on my own, Col, I will curse you from now until the end of time, and your ghost will wander these mountains until they crumble into the sea."

"How poetic," he said. "Been thinking about it much?" He eyed my outstretched hand for a moment, as if weighing the possibility that I was angry enough to send him to his death. "I can do it," he said finally.

"Fine, then, go ahead and die." I watched as Col continued struggling, wondering if I could grab him in case he did fall. I even took a few minutes and ate a snack —days-old bread that I had to pick mold off of. I let Col see me eating, too, and grinned when he huffed out an annoyed breath.

"The offer is still open," I said, holding out my hand. Col sighed and grabbed my arm. With my help, he climbed over the ledge and then rolled to lie beside me for a moment. I was panting with the effort, but nudged him. "And here I thought I was going to have to leave because your arm was healing so fast. Now it looks like you still need my help. Maybe I should stick around."

"And where would you go, Samara?" he asked knowingly. "Would you leave me here and find the alicorn horn on your own?"

I didn't answer for a moment, shocked at the question. Not because it was the truth, but because I hadn't told him any of my thoughts about the artifact. And here Col had seen through me all along.

I recovered my composure and sat up, looking down on him for a change. "And what if I did find it on my own? Would that be so wrong? I wouldn't use it to get rich or stronger, or to gain power. Only to save my little family, to make sure my sister and Da are fed and sheltered. Is that too much to ask?"

Col had been listening quietly. He peered up at me, and I liked how he trusted me enough to be vulnerable like this. Why did he trust me, though? He was on the edge of a cliff with a long drop to the bottom, and he knew I was angry with him, but it didn't faze him.

"It's not too much to ask," he said simply. Then he took a deep breath. "You could have used your power on me anytime during our fight last night. Why didn't you?"

I bit my lip. "I asked myself that same question," I said. "Putting people into an enchanted sleep is my default reaction when I feel threatened."

Col sat up. "And you didn't feel threatened by me."

I shook my head. No, I hadn't.

CHAPTER TWELVE

"I thought these mountains were haunted," I said later.

"They are. With the spirits of the dead who got lost and never returned home."

"Probably because they tried your shortcut," I grumbled.

"You're going to bring all the ghosts down upon us, Samara, if you keep joking like that."

It was the third day of climbing through the mountains. Col still insisted we were going to beat the army to Prismvale, but I had lost all pleasure in looking ahead, instead focusing on where I placed my feet, and trying to hold on to my anger. As we gained elevation, the air became steadily colder. The wind was practically frigid and threatened to tear the skin off my face, so I pulled the hood of the cloak as low as I could and still see.

Col's arm had weakened again, and though a setback wasn't uncommon, it made our journey even more treacherous. Unfortunately, we were running low on the tea I needed to treat him, and we were nowhere near close enough to gathering the ingredients for more.

"We haven't seen anything since we got here, not even any dead bodies or old bones," I said. Apparently, the icy temperatures and blistering wind made my humor darker.

"*You* haven't seen anything," Col said irritably. "But we passed more than one underground entrance, and a few nights I've heard the sound of claws moving over rocks, carried to us on the wind."

I looked back at him, gaping. Then my gaze darted around the pale stone. "Why haven't you said anything before?"

"Because they weren't threats, not yet. It still isn't a good idea to joke about spirits and monsters in these mountains. You never know what you might call up."

"Have you run across them before? It's obvious you've been this way, otherwise we would be hopelessly lost."

We stood on some boulders looking out over the hills, now far away. Smoke still rose ominously from the faraway plain, blotting out the sky to the east. "Once before," Col said. "But I was going in the other direction."

And then he didn't say anything more for several more hours, until night fell and it began to snow.

"There's a place we can camp nearby," Col said. "Somewhere to get out of the storm."

I was going to ask what storm, but then I shook my head. The clouds to the west looked menacing, and the snow was falling harder with every passing minute. I didn't enjoy the idea of spending the night in the open, so I hurried after Col, who was climbing down into a shallow ravine.

A tree emerged from the snowfall, one that still had white shimmering leaves and grew as full and tall as if it were beside a river rather than at the top of a rocky wasteland. It resembled a willow tree, but its bark was darker.

Not just any tree. A "grieving tree." They only grew over the graves of good people, of people who had died premature deaths. According to legend, it was the gods' way of sending comfort, which I thought was a load of horseshit.

On the other side of the tree was a shallow bowl with a slight overhang, which I hurried to tuck myself underneath, next to Col.

"Yes," he said. "Someone died here."

I pictured the cairn I'd raised over Flint—what seemed like months ago now but had really only been a couple of weeks—and wondered if a similar tree would someday grow over his grave.

Col was building a small fire, having dragged enough kindling and wood for just such a night as this one. It was amazing that we'd climbed so far with all the supplies. With the storm now whipping over the mountain, it wouldn't matter if anyone saw the fire or not. They'd never be able to get to us, or so I hoped.

The fire felt amazing, and even though it was small, I hunched over it as close as I dared, letting it heat my face until it was painful. When I sat back, Col was watching me.

"Did you know the person who died here?" I asked softly.

He nodded. "A friend who had grown up with me. We were like brothers. When I came this way last time, he was at my side. But enormous wolves found us that night and surrounded us. We both fought, but the wolves didn't act like a normal pack. They were almost insane in their frenzy—not caring for their own safety but seeking only to overrun us. Almost like they were possessed. I watched my friend fall, and he was dead before I could get to him. In my rage, I slew the rest of the monsters and then tossed their bodies over the cliff edge. This tree is where I built a mound over my friend."

"What was his name?"

"Kiaran."

Tentatively, I put my hand on Col's knee. "I'm sorry."

My throat closed up, and I watched the fire. I was worried about Laney, my father, and Flint's wife, Rose. By now, she would know something bad had happened. We had never been gone this long. I had never left Laney this long.

The urge to leave for home right away almost over-whelmed me. But one look at the snow told me I wasn't going anywhere tonight.

"How many more days?" I asked.

"Ready to be rid of my company?" Col asked gently.

I knew he was teasing, but when I looked up at him, ready to tell him that I wasn't in the mood for his sad jokes, he was gazing at me intently. The firelight bounced off his hazel eyes, making them look more golden than green, and I got lost in them for a moment, indulging myself... and my desire. The feeling shocked me, and I quickly reminded myself that my ass was still sore, and that this man was off-limits even if he didn't use torture as a method of teaching.

Though I couldn't remember why, just then.

I had already realized that I trusted him, but there had been something else holding me back. Something that had to do with his aura of mystery. He knew more about me than I knew about him, and all the flirting over the past few days was a barrier between us, to keep each other at arm's length.

"I'm as eager to leave as you are to be rid of me," I said cryptically, brushing a wayward strand of hair out of my eyes.

"Samara," he said, shifting positions to face me. I went to remove my hand from his knee, but he placed his hand on top of mine.

"Yes?"

Col sat there looking at me for a moment, and I felt a tug in my heart. I wanted to lean forward and caress his worn face, to kiss him—a bad idea. But I waited. "Yes?" I repeated.

"Tomorrow... We should be in Prismvale by tomorrow evening, granted we don't have any delays."

I could have sworn he had been about to say something else, but I nodded, still relishing the feel of his warm hand on top of mine.

"And then what? We ask around for someone whose name and description we don't know?"

"It's our only option. You have a better suggestion?"

I leaned forward just a little, a small shift in my body —that was all the ground I could give him. Col glanced at my lips, and I licked them in anticipation.

He ran his hand up my arm and drew me closer to him, pulling me suddenly so that I was practically straddling his lap. My face was now even with his, and he ran his other hand behind my neck and pulled me close.

Col kissed me.

I put my hands on his chest and leaned in, savoring the taste of him. Everything about him reminded me of good things, fantastic things, things I had never believed in before. That the world was just for me and him, that everything would be all right. I kissed him back, tentatively, and he moved his free hand down my body, letting it rest on my thigh.

"Samara..." he said against my mouth.

But I didn't want to hear what he had to say. I moved in for another kiss, this one deeper, and his tongue sought entrance to my mouth. I opened for him and then pressed my body to his, wanting to feel more of him against me.

Not content with his hand on my thigh, I moved it to my ass. But he pulled back. "You said if I touched your ass again with *any appendage—*"

I took his hand and placed it back on my ass. "I'm giving you permission. Don't screw this up."

Col smiled and kneaded my backside, which practically melted on its own as the still-tender flesh was soothed. As he drew me even closer to him, his grip on me was like a lifeline in the storm that whipped cold air and ice around us. He tethered me to reality but was taking me out of it at the same time. And I didn't know what had changed between us, but I wanted more of it.

I threaded my fingers through his long hair as his tongue plunged deeply into my mouth, over and over. Every touch, even through clothing, was like fire to my body. I ground my hips into his, feeling his erection between us, my body seeking more than I had any right to have.

Then, all too quickly, he let go of me and stilled my hands, which had dropped to his chest and neck.

"Samara, I—"

But I didn't get to hear what he was about to say because he suddenly grabbed my waist and lifted me off him, almost throwing me to the ground. In the same motion, he stood and drew his sword.

The cold from the absence of his body almost made me moan, but I didn't have time to complain. I heard what had caused him to get up and climb out of our shelter.

It was the scrape of claws on stone, close enough to be heard over the sound of the wind, which meant they were close indeed.

Something—a monster—had interrupted us, and I was burning with both embarrassment and anger as I found my own sword.

The weapon suddenly felt clumsy in my hands, but I moved quickly to Col's side, standing next to his right arm and shouting over the wind. "What is it?"

"I'm not sure! Don't leave my side!" He was holding

his sword in his left hand, and I knew that he was skilled with it, but that didn't stop me from trembling, and it wasn't just from the cold. We stood like that for several minutes, with the wind howling in my ears like it was trying to tear me off the mountain.

My night vision finally adjusted, but there wasn't much to see but snow. I pressed my shoulder to Col's and immediately felt better. Where I was trembling, he was calm and assured. And yet there was a tension in him that told me we were not safe.

For a long while, we stared into the darkness, and then I saw something. A shadow that shouldn't have been where it was, even in the dark. I nudged Col with my elbow, and he followed my gaze.

"Don't move," he said. "It can't hear you and has limited scent, but it sees well in the dark. It's looking right at us."

"What is it?"

"A lotimoth. What you see is the shadow of its wings, which is all that it ever shows. They don't come out during the day."

"Fuck," I said.

"Yeah." Suddenly, Col raised his sword and strode forward. "Demon of the night, ghost of the mountains, you are not welcome here!"

Something strange happened. Col's voice rose and grew louder than I'd ever heard a human voice become. It echoed off mountains and sounded worse than the storm itself.

And I was afraid, so afraid that I wanted to throw myself down on the earth so that I didn't have to look at him. With his back to the fire, Col continued shouting like that for a long while, showing his sword and creating general chaos in the air. The wind carried his voice until it echoed all around us in a way that could not possibly be natural.

With a shudder, I realized Col had magic of his own.

At one point, a black feather drifted in front of my face before being whipped away on the wind, and I cried out, thinking there was another lotimoth somewhere above us. But Col's voice didn't change, and nothing attacked.

After a long time, he stopped shouting and lowered his sword. I was gaping at him.

"It's gone," he said, retrieving a cup from the baggage and sweeping snow into it. Then he put it over the fire.

"You're safe, Samara," he said finally, looking up into my eyes.

I was shaking from head to toe and had no idea why. If Col said the lotimoth was gone, I believed him, and yet... His very presence unnerved me now. It took me a moment to get control of myself and move to sit by the fire. I groaned as its warmth washed over me, and got as close as I dared without setting myself on fire.

Col grabbed his cloak, abandoned when he went to confront the lotimoth, and tossed it over me. Then he began rubbing my back and tucking the cloak all the way around my body, even the hood, so that nothing was exposed to the air. When he covered my eyes, I laughed, and the act released the tension in my body. I tried to look up at him, but he was behind me, rubbing my back. When the snow in the cup was melted and warm, he wrapped the cup in a cloth and handed it to me.

"Careful," he said. "It's hot."

I laughed again. It seemed like such a simple thing to say after what had just happened. Col continued rubbing my back while I sipped the hot water, wishing it were tea but knowing that we didn't have anything except for his medicine. It warmed me, though, and that was the important thing.

"How did you . . .?" I asked as he wrapped his arm around me. "What *was* that?"

Col slowed the hand on my back. Wrapped up so fully, I could barely move, let alone twist to see his face. I could feel his steady, even breathing, though, his chest rising and falling against my shoulder. Finally, I pulled down the hood and looked up at him. "Col?"

When he didn't answer, I shoved the cup at him. "You have magic. I showed you mine, Col. It's only fair for you to show me yours."

He laughed, then, but there was still a remnant of that magic left in his voice, and it caused me to shudder.

Finally, he took the cup, put more snow in it, and placed it back on the fire.

"It's something that's always been in my family," he said. "I can't tell you where it came from because I don't know. As far as I'm aware, it's not quite like your ability. It's not due to some other people's blood in my veins. And I can't use it all the time. Only in times of great need, and even then it doesn't always appear."

"And it works on monsters?"

He shook his head. "Not all. Only on sentient ones, those that know what they are."

I tilted my head. "Even a bird knows that it is a bird."

"True. But it wouldn't work on just any stupid beast. I first discovered I could use it that night my friend Kiaran died, when the demon wolves tore him apart." Col paused, and when he spoke again, his voice was quiet. "That's also the night I discovered my father was dead. Because the magic is only something that awakens in a male heir once the head of our family has died. In the end, it worked too late to save my friend because I hesitated. The knowledge that I'd lost my father... well, it shocked me even though it shouldn't have."

I truly didn't know what to say. I was dumbstruck, even though I had some experience with voice magic.

"Why didn't you use it on the soldier when we captured him?"

"I didn't need to. He was desperate enough to get away that he would have said anything. And if I had used it, I could have opened us up to worse. If the information had got back to The Harrow that I was alive and hunting his men, we might not have survived, even up here."

So much information, but it never seemed enough. My curiosity was piqued instead of sated. "The Harrow knows you?"

Col nodded curtly, and a muscle worked in his jaw. "We've met."

"How?"

"He killed my parents."

I sat there, struck mute once again at the revelation.

"It was years ago," Col continued, "and I would give up every trace of magic if it meant they were alive again."

I nodded. That was something I understood very deeply. I would do anything to have my mother and brother back. And Flint. I swallowed the lump in my throat. "And that thing you can do when you know someone's lying?"

"That's not magic, just a long history of being around liars." Col smiled. "Don't worry, Samara, I haven't been hoodwinking you into helping me."

I smiled. "*Have* you used compulsion on people before?"

He shook his head. "It doesn't work like that. It's more like eliciting an emotional response from someone when I tell them what to do. I tried, on you, when we first met. I'm ashamed to admit it now."

I gazed into his eyes, remembering how I had reacted when he'd first captured me. How I'd felt like it would be the most wonderful thing in the world to obey him. But the feeling had vanished. "You stopped doing it."

"You were strong, and it was going to take a lot of power to subdue you." He took my hand, and still finding it cold, began to rub it. "And I didn't want to. I don't like using it, if I'm honest."

But tonight... Why had I wanted to throw myself to the ground? Was it because even though the magic wasn't meant for me, there was some sort of residual effect?

"I'm sorry if I scared you."

When I looked back at him, I saw that he was sincere. I was starting to feel better now, the cloak, the fire, and the hot water doing their job. Still, I couldn't resist tucking myself closer to his warm body.

A sword passed down through generations, and now magic. *Who are you, Col?*

I was going to ask, but he said, "Thank you, Samara."

"What are you thanking me for this time?" I asked, too comfortable and sleepy to move.

"For trusting me."

Before I fell asleep, I wondered if I'd even had a choice.

CHAPTER THIRTEEN

"**A**re you sure you haven't been using your power on me?" I asked the next day, and then inwardly cringed. I had a right to ask the question, yet I had promised myself I wouldn't. Col had been subdued all day, speaking little and moving quickly. And though the behavior was normal, it felt strange.

We were finally leaving the most difficult terrain behind, but it was still a place to watch every step. Going down was every bit as treacherous as going up. Thankfully, the snowstorm had passed so we didn't have to shout at each other, and we'd already descended below the worst of the snowdrifts.

Col glanced back at me. "Of course not." His voice was raw and scratchy, and he was having more trouble with his arm. "Do you know what to do for a sore throat? Another magic tea, perhaps?"

"Sure, if I can find the ingredients." I shrugged. "Although it's not magic, just knowledge."

"And what will I owe you, when this is all over?"

I grinned, though his back was too me. "All magic has a cost."

"And what is the cost of yours?" Col stopped walking and turned to me.

"I'll think of something." I smiled.

He nodded, and we continued.

What is the cost? The question lingered in my mind, bringing up unpleasant memories, and new worries.

There had always been a cost for using my magic. I had often been shunned, and my parents had kept me from the eyes of others until I learned to control it. What was sometimes a gift was always a curse. A curse I was ready to break. I wanted to be normal.

I chuckled quietly to myself as I skidded down an incline, only to scramble over a boulder at the bottom. Maybe "normal" was taking things too far. Normal was boring. But I wanted to be human, and free.

We didn't talk for the rest of the day, saving our energy for the long hike downward. Below us was a lush green valley, a fertile swath of land between two tall mountain ranges. This was the edge of The Harrow's lands, a kingdom in which I had lived so long that the thought of crossing into somewhere else filled me with both dread and excitement.

The closer we got to the valley floor, the more careful Col became. We avoided any roads and even the scattering of houses built into the mountainside. Finally, I got my first glimpse of Prismvale. What I had thought would be a village was more of a small city, with high wooden walls and a small keep near the river that divided the valley.

But that was all I saw before we descended into the trees and reached the valley floor. There was farmland and industry, and I was surprised to find it at the borderlands. What was usually ruin elsewhere had turned into opportunity here. Col explained that Prismvale was home to many smiths who armed Harrowfell's soldiers, and sometimes the rebel soldiers on the sly.

"Of course," he continued, "anyone caught helping the enemy is killed very slowly and painfully. But there's enough money in it that most armorers and blacksmiths will risk it if they think they can get away with it."

Eventually, we entered the road, the only way into the city.

I had never been anywhere with so many people, but the stench drifting over the place wasn't the normal stench of humans living together. It was the stench of decay and rot, and I looked up at the wall as we approached it. Spikes stuck out from it every few feet, and each one had a head on it. They were in various states of decay, some with long hair, some with short, some with no hair, and some of those so young they hadn't even had a chance to choose. I shuddered and looked away, wondering what kind of monster would kill a young child. But I knew the answer.

It was The Harrow and his minions. It was always them.

Col had been here before, and he took my hand at the gates. His sure grip was warm and comforting in the throng of people. This time of day, the gates were thrown open, with the guards outside looking us over but not stopping us.

The name of Prismvale suggested it was a city of elves, but if they had ever lived here, their influence was long gone. My first impression of the city, other than its stench, was how muddy everything was. Mud on the few stone buildings, on the horses, the people. Everywhere.

Wagons, horses, and people pressed through, jostling us to the side, and it looked like many of them were trying to leave for the day.

"They close the gates at night," Col explained. "And we better find shelter before nightfall. The city isn't safe at the best of times, but it's not a place to wander in the dark."

He led us down one alley, then another, all while wending our way closer to the heart of the city. We didn't see many soldiers, only city guards. Peacekeepers, they were called. The heads on the outer walls told me what kind of "peace" they kept. As we came to a three-story inn next door to a tavern, I wondered how in all the kingdoms we were going to find our thief.

"It doesn't look as if the soldiers are here yet," Col said at the door. "But we still need to be on our guard. Don't talk to strangers, and don't cause any trouble."

"I fended for myself for a long time before I met you, Col."

He chuckled. "I don't doubt that, but it's better not to draw any attention to ourselves whatsoever, especially with your..." He lowered his voice so I had to strain to hear him. "Ability. Best not to let anyone know who or what we are."

I nodded. It was easy enough to understand, and I

had no intention of drawing attention to myself. "Are we staying here?" I asked, looking at the sign on the inn.

Col nodded. "One room?" he asked. "Or two?"

The heat in his eyes must have been echoed in my own. "One, I think," he said before I answered. "To make sure you stay out of trouble."

I swallowed, hard. We'd been sleeping near each other outdoors for weeks now, ridden the same horse with our bodies pressed together, but the thought of spending time with him in a room, with a bed, made my heart beat a strange tempo against my chest. "Two rooms," I countered, with less conviction than I'd hoped.

As it turned out, there was only one room available, so I didn't have a choice. After Col paid, we went next door to get some food. There was a large hearth with a blazing fire to ward off the chill of the night, and I downed a whole roast fowl by myself before sopping up the juices with a large piece of bread. It was more than I'd ever eaten in one sitting, and I was so full that I had to sit back and put my hands on my belly. Though at one time too much food had made me sick, while traveling with Col, I had not gone hungry, and I had grown used to regular meals. We rationed our food but there always seemed to be enough, and I wondered about that. Watching Col tuck in to his own dinner, I wondered if he had been eating less so that I could have more.

The thought made me a bit queasy, so I sat up and studied him a bit more closely. Had his shoulder been slow to heal because he wasn't eating enough? He didn't look thinner than when I had met him, but I hadn't really been paying that much attention in those early days.

"I think I'm going to need to loosen my trousers, I ate so much." I grinned wickedly at Col, who just shook his head. There were a few other patrons around us, all of them minding their own business, which was just as well. There was a bartender, and I beckoned him to bring two flagons of ale. When Col saw them, he raised an eyebrow but didn't say anything.

A woman brought the ale and placed one in front of each of us. I drank mine eagerly, draining the flagon and setting it down with a sigh.

Col was enjoying his too, albeit much more slowly. "One of us needs to keep our wits," he said with a smile.

After a while, and in my case feeling more satisfied than I had in a long time, years even, we went up to our room. It was small, with a double bed and a mattress that looked like it had been recently stuffed. I sighed and sank down on it without even thinking, groaning at feeling the pillow under my head.

"Careful there, love. It looks like you're getting ready to come."

I burst out laughing and sat up, shocked that Col had made such a remark. He smirked, and after placing our things near the door, he pulled the latch down to lock it. There was a washbasin, and I hurried to splash water over my face, hoping he didn't see my cheeks flush or hear my heart pounding wildly. Then, I made an effort to braid my hair for the first time in ages. Feeling not quite clean but better, I looked down at my clothes. They were filthy, and I loathed the idea of sleeping in them again, especially in a bed.

There was a knock on the door, and when Col

opened it, it was the innkeeper's wife, asking if we had any washing. She did it overnight, she said, and it only cost a few coppers. I had never been happier to hear Col say yes. Quickly, without even caring about modesty, I stripped out of everything. I was so glad to think of clean clothes that I wrapped the bedsheet around me, bundled up everything else, and gave the laundry to the woman before Col had even begun undressing.

"You smell," I said teasingly.

With a chuckle, he began removing his armor and then clothes, and I had to stop myself from staring at his chiseled, rock-hard features that *did* look a bit thinner than when I had met him. His right shoulder had a savage pink scar that was barely healed over, and the dark raven tattoo depicted in flight on his left breast looked as if it was pointing at the injury. Without warning, Col stripped off his pants as well, and I turned away, not because I wasn't curious, but so the innkeeper's wife wouldn't see me blushing. She didn't even bat an eye when, completely naked, he handed over his clothes, said good night, and closed the door.

I sat on the bed facing away from him as I listened to him washing.

"I wonder if they have a bathtub," I said, half to myself.

"Maybe tomorrow," he said. "We have to get up early and need to get some sleep."

I knew he was right, but the thought of being in this room with a naked man who had such an amazing body was doing things to my common sense. Finally, I tossed him the blanket, making a point not to look too low.

Col smiled as he wrapped it around his waist. "I don't mind if you look, Samara," he said. I grinned but kept looking at the wall.

I really wanted to do much more than look at him, but it was best to not even tempt myself. This was a man I barely knew, who had a strange power of compulsion with his voice, and I needed to keep my head on straight. We hadn't even talked about that kiss, like it had never happened. It had been a mistake, anyway, I told myself.

Liar. The heat that pooled in my lower body at just the thought of kissing him had me pressing my thighs together.

I lay on the bed, keeping my face to the wall. After a moment, Col climbed in beside me and threw half the blanket over me. Knowing that he was lying there naked, I reminded myself how dirty I was, and that there was no way I was going to allow anything to happen before I had a proper bath. With this thought in mind, the exhaustion coupled with the softness of the bed did their work, and I quickly fell asleep.

Our clothes were waiting outside our door the next day, and although I had woken wanting more than anything to feel Col's hands on me, I washed from the basin and dressed in a hurry because it was cold. He was already dressed and waiting outside the door, and when I opened it, I grinned and felt shy for some reason.

"Let's get this over with," he said.

He was dreading this search as much as me. We had a whole city to comb, and very little time to do it. I didn't know when the soldiers would arrive, but they would not take as long as I wanted them to. If they never came, I would be happy.

The first thing we did was stop by the tavern. They were serving a cold breakfast of meat and buttered bread, but we only paid for the bread. As we ate, Col asked the serving woman about any travelers, but got no useful information.

"I guess it couldn't have been that easy," I said when the door shut behind us. When we left the tavern, the sun was peeking over the distant wall, but it wasn't warming the air. The city was smoky and smelly, and I longed for the comfort of that bed again.

"Indeed."

"Where to now?" I asked.

"I don't think the inn is the place to be. If the thief were coming here, he—"

"Or she, or they—"

Col nodded. "If they came to Prismvale, it's probably because they had a connection. They're going to pass our item off to someone here, sell it maybe. And we know it's not The Harrow's soldiers because he's sending an army to get it."

"If the thief came here," I said, "it might be to help a cause, right? To help the rebels... or Glimmerdale's elves. Who is currently standing up against Harrowfell in this area?"

"Good question. I don't know for certain, but I know exactly who to ask."

"The blacksmiths?"

"The blacksmiths. But first," he said, tugging my hand, "we have another errand."

THE "ERRAND" was finding new clothing for me. I gaped when he took me into a shop full of nice clothes hanging on racks and folded on a long counter. The woman behind it greeted us as we walked in.

But I turned to Col. "Why?" I asked.

He looked irritated. "Because you nearly froze in those mountains, and your clothes are only fit for the trash pile."

"I meant why are *you* buying them?"

"Do you have any money?"

I shook my head, slightly ashamed. "You know I don't."

"But I do," he said, "and I can't think of anything I'd rather spend it on than some new clothes for you."

I looked him over, at his black clothes that looked worse for wear but had been made to hold up. At his leather armor and fine belt and cloak. "I don't want your charity," I whispered.

Col took my arm and gently steered me toward the counter. "It's not charity. Think of it as a partial repayment for all you have done for me."

"Only partial?"

He smirked. "Just pick out some clothes, will you? Whatever you like, but make sure they are practical."

I had only ever worn practical clothes. The thought of wearing anything else hadn't even crossed my mind. I browsed the folded clothes and spent some time chatting with the clerk, who had been looking at my current ensemble with a critical eye.

The clothes I picked out were practical, but they were also the nicest things I'd ever owned, though Col said they were "okay" when I showed him. The clerk measured me to make some alterations, Col paid her, and then we left the shop.

I felt awkward about the exchange. Col had spent practically all his money on my clothes, and we didn't know how long we would be in Prismvale. But when I brought it up, he merely shrugged. "I can always find work if needed. But I've lived on the road long enough to know how to stretch what I have."

He threw an arm around my shoulders and steered me away from the shop. "Let me take care of you, for a change."

As we began our search for the thief, I wondered if he'd been taking care of me all along.

WE SPENT the rest of the day visiting various armorers and blacksmiths, asking how the war was going. And because it was the sort of thing a spy might ask, most of them were eager to tell of The Harrow's victories. Of course, no one would admit that there were any enemies or spies within the city walls, even though it was likely. Still, we learned easily enough, and from several different sources, that the kingdom of Glimmerdale had been pushing back against Harrowfell for months now, and that The Harrow had been sending soldiers out from here.

"Do any of the elves come into the city?" I asked.

The blacksmith, an enormous man that looked like he could be part troll, studied me for a moment. "I reckon it's possible, but of course I have not had any dealings with them." He bowed slightly.

"Of course not, worthy man," Col said. The blacksmith nodded to us, and we left.

"If I were from Glimmerdale," I said, "and I had stolen a magical item, why would I be here and what would I be doing?"

We paused in the street, stepping around a cart headed in the opposite direction. Col waited until its driver was out of earshot before following up. "It's an interesting thought. I'd almost wish Glimmerdale luck in their venture, but I won't rest until I know the horn can't be used for anyone else. Even the elves will go to extremes to defend their kingdom."

"Can't blame them, really."

"No." He thought for a minute. "Only the mages can do something with what we seek. At least, on the scale that would be needed for warfare."

I shuddered. "Deviants."

"If they are with Glimmerdale, they are from a different order, but few mages have it in them to show compassion and mercy."

The last thing I wanted was to get tangled up with any mages, Deviants or not. But I asked anyway. "So do we look for the mages? Where do they hang out?"

Col shook his head. "They don't hang out anywhere. Most of the time they come and go in secret."

"So our thief may either be a mage or be on his way to meet one. How will we ever find them?" Once again, I felt as if I was doing nothing except get farther from home.

"We just keep asking questions," Col said resolutely.

We stomped around the city for the rest of the day, with little luck. Although we had no outright clashes, a few of the blacksmiths and innkeepers we visited glared at us and refused to answer questions. The city was wary of strangers, and I wondered how many people we talked to thought we were spies.

By the time night fell, we hadn't learned anything else. We had visited every inn and tavern in the city, and almost every blacksmith. All of them said the same—that Glimmerdale had tried to send raiders through this valley several times in the past month, and that they were The Harrow's most pressing concern on this border.

I sighed. "The Harrow thinks everybody outside his kingdom is concerning, *and* the ones in it."

"Correct, but Glimmerdale is notorious for its warlords. Their people don't necessarily recognize one king, but don't mind working together to overcome a threat. And they're brutal fighters. I have no problem believing they are The Harrow's chief concern right now. And if they were to get a powerful weapon? Anyone within a thousand leagues of this land might as well start digging their own graves."

"At least they seem the most likely to have our item," I said, mindful of the people still hanging around. "And it explains why they were able to steal it right out from under The Harrow's mage."

"Yes, the Glimmerdale elves are cunning and fierce."

"Have you had any experience with them?"

"Quite a bit. You?"

I shook my head. "None, really."

Before we ate dinner, we went back to pick up my new clothes. The clerk smiled when I put them on in a curtained off room behind the counter, and she hurried away with my old clothes as if she couldn't wait to burn them. When I finished dressing, I stepped out and looked in her glass mirror to see for myself.

What struck me first wasn't the image of the new clothes, but of my appearance. Despite the hardships of the last few weeks, the dark circles under my eyes were gone. My cheeks were fuller from my recent meals, and I had a bit of rosy color in my face, even if my faint greenish undertone made me cringe. I had never been curvy, but with regular meals, my muscles had grown stronger and my body had taken on a lean, fit appearance.

The clothes were finer and more expensive than anything I'd ever owned. I felt guilty wearing them, but then I reminded myself I could always sell them later, if I needed to.

A dark pair of breeches were comfortable and hugged my body in all the right places, but they wouldn't restrict me from riding a horse or climbing. A gray shirt that fell straight and was cinched with my belt, and it flowed over my upper body without a lot of extra fabric to get in the way. New leather boots completed the ensemble, and I blushed when Col looked at me over my shoulder.

"Beautiful," he murmured.

I playfully hit his arm and then moved away from the mirror. "You just like that I'm wearing black now and match you."

"One more thing," he said, and gestured to the clerk again. She brought out a new long, black cloak lined with dark fur. He took it from her and draped it over my shoulders.

"Col, it's too much!"

"You need it. That threadbare cloak wasn't going to last much longer."

I spun to look at him. "How did you..." My gaze glanced at his left hand. His ring was gone. Not the one with the raven, but the other one that had belonged to his mother, the ruby encircled with golden branches. My eyes filled with tears. "No."

Col smiled. "It's just a ring."

"It's not just a ring. It's—"

He took both sides of the cloak and used them to pull me close. "Listen to me. The ring meant something to me, but this means more. It's a fitting trade." Col brushed a kiss over my lips. "My mother was a wonderful, strong woman, but she is gone. And you are here. Let me give you this." He wiped a tear from my cheek. "Please, little songbird?"

I took a deep breath and pulled the cloak around me. It was warm enough that the chill in the air didn't even register. Afraid that my voice was going to crack, I nodded to Col, whose tender kiss was still burning on my lips. I could never seem to refuse him when he said please.

He took my hand and steered me toward our inn, and I watched him out of the corner of my eye. Who was he? I had never met anyone like him. He was the most dangerous man I had ever met, and the most giving. Stern and tender at the same time, and I felt safe with him.

And confused. He obviously had a secret to keep and didn't trust me with it.

We entered the tavern next to our inn and ordered food. This time I didn't even hesitate and ordered two flagons of ale, both for me. Something else had been bothering me, and I didn't wait to swallow a mouthful before asking, "A thousand leagues all around are in danger?"

Col leaned forward. "Or worse."

A chill went through me, and for the first time I understood just how important our errand was. Before, the threat had felt distant, like it was someone else's problem and not mine. I had been wrong. It was still Col's mission, but I was wrapped up in it now, and I couldn't separate his need for it from mine.

We both ate, but my appetite was failing. Col had tight lines across his face but said nothing as he reached across the table for my second tankard of ale and drained it.

"We'll have two more here," I said, gesturing to the serving woman. A different person from the night before.

She gladly brought two more ales over and lingered at the table. She wore a tight dress, one that went to the floor but accentuated all her womanly curves, including a neckline that plunged down to show off her... attributes.

I wondered if they helped her sell more ale, and when I looked around, I realized the room was more crowded tonight, with mostly men. She was obviously trying to catch Col's eye, but he dug into his food and ignored her. Rolling my eyes and laughing a little, I thanked her for the ale and then set about drinking as if I didn't have a care in the world.

Or, more realistically, as if the weight of the entire world was on my shoulders.

CHAPTER FOURTEEN

I lost count of my drinks after three, and the world became infinitely nicer. The fire in the hearth was cheerier, the food tasted better, and my companion became delicious-er.

I invented that word but it was fine since I didn't plan on saying it aloud.

Col seemed to find my drinking amusing, so I urged him to have another, as well, and then another. He didn't put up much of a fight, and soon we were both laughing at nothing and generally feeling good about ourselves and how smart we were.

Smart enough to find a dead end in a city far from home.

But we didn't talk about that. Mostly, he teased me for the way I still held my sword, and I teased him for having a song about his. So, the usual. The butterflies that had been swirling in my stomach disappeared, and I forgot about the sacrifice Col had made for me, and focused instead on the curve of his mouth when he

189

smiled, on the golden flecks in his eyes and the long dark hair that framed his face.

A traveling bard thrummed his lute and began to sing. It was a melancholy tune, and not sung very well, but it somehow was perfect for the tavern. A little rough around the edges and simple, like the bland food, but warm and inviting anyway.

When I stood to get the bartender's attention, I wobbled a bit and ended up leaning on a seated Col. He wrapped an arm around my waist. "Careful. You don't want someone to take advantage of you."

"Someone like you?" I said with a small giggle. I tried to tap the end of his nose with my finger and ended up poking him in the eye instead.

His eye watered as he cursed at me. I just laughed. "Sorry," I whispered with a blush.

The room was swaying now, but I reached over to pick up my tankard, which was still half full of ale. Bringing it to my mouth this time took a little more effort, but I managed to guzzle the rest down, all while leaning on Col, who still had his arm around my waist.

I didn't mind the proximity, and with the alcohol, I even dared to feel bold about our situation. I slammed the tankard down on the table and wiped my mouth with the back of my hand, still giggling. Col finished his and stood suddenly. Keeping a hand on my waist, he leaned down to whisper in my ear. "Dance with me."

Sure on his feet where I was a bit tipsy, he twirled me around the floor, between tables and over to the small empty space in front of the bard. The man nodded his head and sang louder, which didn't improve the song, but drowned out some raucous laughter from a table nearby.

Col pulled me close. All the while, his hand had not left my waist. His other held my left hand on his chest. I gazed into his eyes and my cheeks grew hot. It was from the ale, I told myself, and not from the way he was looking at me. Like I was the only person in the world just then. The background and even the music faded away, and I wrapped my arms around his neck.

We danced close, our bodies moving to the music, not caring who saw us. His cheek was on my cheek, his breath on my ear, and I would be perfectly happy for this night to never end. To just stay in Col's arms and forget the world outside, to just be a normal human with normal human problems.

A sudden flush of guilt washed over me, amplified by the drink and the music. No matter how much I wished it, I was not human. I was a filthy half-breed. And Col... well, I didn't know who he was.

And Laney was at home. At least, I hoped she was safe in the bog, which felt a world away right now. And for all intents and purposes, it was.

"Everything okay?" Col murmured against my cheek. I realized I had stopped moving with him. I pulled back to look at him, and some of my own pain and guilt were reflected in his eyes. Was he giving it a second thought? Did he regret trading his mother's ring for a cloak for a half-breed?

I looked away, unable to handle that intense gaze of his that seemed to see right through me. One day soon, I imagined, he would wake up and realize who he was dancing with, and then where would that leave me?

"Hey," he said, cupping my chin. I pulled away out of his arms and made my way back to the table, trying not to notice the stares that were coming my way.

Col followed, getting the bartender's attention as he sat. "I'm tired of ale. Let's drink something stronger."

I had never tried goblin whiskey before, had never heard of it, in fact, but it burned my throat all the way down.

I had three. It had been a long time since I'd let go, and once I started I couldn't stop. I just wanted to forget everything for a while.

"Want another," I said, slurring my words. I raised my hand again to get the bartender's attention.

Col stood and took my arm. "I'm pretty sure we've both had enough."

At least that's what I think he said, but his words were somewhat slurred, too. Or maybe my hearing was slurred. I pouted—playfully, I hoped. "You're no fun. You broody moody dutiful deliciouser man."

I was gazing up into Col's eyes, noticing how the flecks of gold really stood out in the firelight. I was still leaning heavily on him, my shoulder pressed into his chest with his arm around me. "Moody broody," I repeated with a laugh that turned into a gasp.

"And you, Samara, are my broody queen." He laughed, too, almost losing his own balance, and I snaked my arm around his waist. To support him, obviously.

"I'd like a bath," I said.

He laughed even harder, as if it was the funniest

thing he'd ever heard. "I'd better go with you," he said loudly, "to make sure you don't drown. You're drunk."

We both laughed as we swayed and stumbled our way out of the tavern. I caught some looks as we left, people who seemed to be laughing at us, but everything was funny tonight, wasn't it?

We went next door to our inn, and Col snagged the innkeeper's wife. "Bath please. And candles."

His accent was funnier than usual, but the innkeeper's wife only rolled her eyes. "I'll have Simon bring the tub up to your room. It'll be a few minutes. You're not the only people in the inn, you know."

We both laughed at that, and she left in a huff. Col turned me so we faced the stairs, and I glared at them. "How the hell are we going to get up those?" I asked.

"You're drunker than I am." In a fit of valor, Col tried to pick me up and lift me over his shoulder. But he barely got me up there before he stumbled against the wall and banged my head.

"Ow."

"Sorry." He set me back on my feet, and we fell over against the same wall, sliding down it until we were in sitting positions.

"Okay," I said, rubbing my head. "New plan. We have our bath down here."

"By the door?" Col asked and then sniggered loudly. "Then everyone will see us."

I shook my head. "I don't care."

I was feeling a little sick from all the spinning the room was doing.

Col managed to get to his feet, grabbed both of my

hands, and pulled me up. "Come on love, I'll get you up there."

And then, wrapping an arm around my waist and putting another hand on the railing, Col began to half drag me up the stairs. He told me which foot to move and helped me place one in front of the other, and though he wasn't much better off than I, after a few painful minutes, we were standing at the top of the stairs. I got on my hands and knees and began crawling toward our door.

"What are you doing that for?" he asked, wobbling dangerously.

"I don't want to fall down the stairs."

"Good point." He got on his hands and knees, too, and finally, we made it to our room, which already had a tub in it.

"'S magic," I said, pointing.

We sat shoulder-to-shoulder against the wall while we watched the innkeeper's wife and sturdy son come in with buckets of hot water. "Hey!" I yelled at them. "How'd you get up here so fast, huh?"

The innkeeper's wife sighed. "We used the back stair, honey. If we'd waited for you two to get your asses up here, our suppers would be cold."

Col barked a laugh.

"And where are the candles?" I slurred.

"No candles tonight," said the woman. "We don't want you to burn the place down."

Col and I both giggled hysterically at that.

The room filled with steam, but I was already hot with liquid courage. I began pulling off my clothes before the door closed for the final time.

"Waitwaitwaitwait wait," Col said. He scooched over to the door and put the latch down. "There. Now no one will come in."

I giggled for some reason, then shed all my clothes and fell into the warm bath with a big splash. The water was so hot I thought it was going to burn my skin, but then I got used to it, and relaxed with my head against the back of the tub.

I hadn't cared that Col saw me naked, and when he began to undress, I openly watched him.

When he removed his shirt, I saw the same chiseled muscles and golden skin. When he removed his pants, I couldn't help but watch. His cock bobbed up and down as he discarded his last bit of clothing, and I stared at it for a long time. It was huge.

Finally, I met his eyes, which were as intense as ever. "You're a hard man," I said with a snort. At this point I didn't even know what was funny and what wasn't.

Col slipped into the other end of the bath and entwined his legs with mine. "This way you can't drown," he said with an attempt at a wink. Then he laid his head back against the tub and sighed deeply.

I watched him for a moment and then laid my head back too. The room was still spinning, but the water made me feel as if I was floating in a warm cocoon. I closed my eyes, and the hot water began to do its work. It was scented with something, and I relaxed even more as the tension and days of travel eased out of my body.

I thought to tell Col that I wanted something, but I suddenly couldn't remember what it was. All I could register was the hot water and the weight of his legs tangled in mine. His skin was rough where mine was smooth, and I thought about his arm and the way he had been able to use it tonight, to get me up the stairs. I laughed again at how funny it was that the ale had healed his arm.

There was something not quite right about that, but I brushed the inkling aside in favor of running my foot up and down his thigh. My toe bumped something else of his, and I giggled. He was still so big, and, watching to see what would happen, I spread my toes and used them to grab his length. Then I began to stroke him with my feet, splashing water all over the floor.

His cock grew bigger.

In the moment, it felt like an erotic thing to do, and I fantasized about seducing Col, about straddling him right here in the tub and sinking down onto that hard man flesh of his and riding him until the water all splashed out of the tub.

Col said something, but I was becoming more disengaged by the minute. Finally, I realized I'd stopped stroking him.

Then, relaxed and completely drunk, I looked up and saw Col looking at me.

CHAPTER FIFTEEN

The next time I opened my eyes, my head was pounding. Slowly, the room came into focus, and the light through the small window felt like someone was stabbing my eyeballs with a pick. I groaned and pulled the sheet up over my body.

That's when I noticed the arm wrapped around my waist.

And the naked flesh pressed against my back.

Along with another bit of velvety flesh that seemed to be resting between my thighs.

My eyes flew open again, and I lifted the sheet.

I was naked with Col's strong arm wrapped around me, his left hand holding my breast. For a moment, I tried to think about why we were lying together naked in the bed, but part of me wanted to just stay there.

Then I remembered the drinking. I remembered taking a bath with him, too, and... fondling him with my feet.

Oh goddess. What had I done? Oh goddess. If he

remembered, I'd just like the ground to open up and take me down to the Bitter Realms right now.

Groaning with mortification, I grabbed his wrist and pulled his hand away from my breast, and cold air rushed in to replace it. It made my nipple peak, and if my head hadn't been pounding so badly, it would have been pleasurable. I extricated myself from the bed, taking the sheet with me. I had no idea where the other blankets were, and then I looked on the floor.

Oh.

The blankets had been tossed on the floor, which was soaked with water.

What had we done? I didn't know. I mean, I didn't feel like I'd... The towels lay on the chair, unused, and I supposed we had just crawled into bed wet.

What else had we done?

My new clothes lay on the floor where I'd tossed them. Thankfully, they had escaped the drowning that affected the rest of the room.

Finally, my gaze went back to the bed and Col's large sleeping form. He was naked and uncovered, since I had the sheet, and even through the haze of my hangover, I could admire how beautiful his body was, how strong and powerful it looked even in sleep. His thigh muscles were chiseled like the rest of him, and when he moved just a little, the light fell on him, showing off even more of his body's contours.

Contours that led to a happy trail of hair leading down his belly, to...

He was fully erect, and part of me—the very, very

naughty part of me—wanted to go over and do something about that.

But I could barely make it over to the washbasin, where I stumbled, feeling sick. Dunking a cloth in the cold water, I ran it over my face and neck, feeling hot and woozy and turned on all the same time. I didn't think that was possible.

"Hey," I said, checking if he was awake. I thought about getting dressed and sneaking out before he saw me, but I knew I wouldn't be able to get down the stairs in my current state. How had we even gotten upstairs last night?

It was a miracle we hadn't killed ourselves. Either that, or I had been much more drunk than he was.

Looking at his form again, I realized I really, really needed to know what happened. Because if we'd... If we had sex, I had things I needed to think about. I needed a tea, a different kind from the one I'd been giving Col. And I needed coin to pay someone for the ingredients since we were nowhere near a place to gather them myself—I sank down on the bed and groaned.

The bed creaked behind me, and I instantly regretted my sudden movement. "You awake?" I whispered.

"Yeah," he said hoarsely. There was a subtle intake of breath as he took in the state of the messy room. "By the goddess, what happened?"

"What did we do last night?" I asked. That I had no real memory of anything after the bath was starting to feel like a dumb joke.

"A-apparently, we took a bath? All I remember was you asking the bartender for more ale."

"I remember you ordering something stronger than ale..."

He groaned and sank onto the mattress, which shifted with his weight. Gingerly, I glanced behind me—to see his face, that was all. "You don't remember?" I asked. I didn't believe him, not one bit. But then, I didn't remember anything myself. Had we done something and he was keeping it from me? Would he tell me?

"Col?"

"I don't remember," he said, rubbing his eyes and then putting his hand over his face. "I mean, I wouldn't have taken advantage of you—you were very drunk." He mumbled something. "And so was I."

Carefully, I crawled out of bed, still a little drunk, and keeping the sheet wrapped firmly under my arms. "Do you feel like... Do you feel like you did anything?"

Col removed his hand from his face and gave me a puzzled look. "What do you mean?"

I glanced down at his still very erect member, which was practically waving at me from between those hard, muscled thighs. I gulped. He was enormous.

"By the gods, Samara, I'm not even sure my head is still attached to my shoulders, let alone what else happened last night."

Tearing my eyes away from his cock—*his hard, gigantic cock*—I looked into his eyes.

But then he sat up and turned his back toward me, reaching for his pants lying not too far away. He pulled them on, fastened them, and then turned back around. "How do you feel?" he asked hesitantly. "Do you feel like... anything happened?"

I shook my head and instantly regretted it when the room began spinning.

Col chuckled to himself. "Well then it's all right, isn't it?"

I raised an eyebrow.

He smirked. "Because, my little songbird, if you and I had done something in that bed other than sleep, you would barely be walking this morning."

Even in my current state of unwellness, I blushed. Full-on blushed like a teenager talking to her first crush. Turning away with a silent curse, I reached for my clothes.

Col rubbed his hand over his face. "I just can't seem to stop," he mumbled. Then he sighed and dropped his hand. "Forget I said anything, okay?"

"You're awkward the morning after—noted," I muttered, pulling on my clothes while keeping the sheet around me. The sooner we were dressed, the sooner we could leave and find some food, or perhaps another ale… for the terrible hangover.

We didn't speak as we gathered our things, anything to keep from jostling my head around, and from the way Col moved, he felt the same. My hair had dried in wild waves, and I tried to tame it with another braid, but struggled to get very far. Even my scalp hurt.

"Here," said Col. He had come up behind me and put his hands on mine. I dropped my hands and let him deal with the crazy locks, feeling too sick to care what he did. In a few moments, he had carefully finger-combed the tangles and then smoothed my hair into a loose braid that he arranged over my shoulder.

"You can braid hair?" I asked as I inspected it.

"Just something I picked up." Col gathered his own shoulder-length waves behind his head and tied them back. "Ready?"

Throwing my satchel and other things over my shoulder made me woozy.

Don't throw up don't throw up don't throw up!

I was not going to puke in front of Col, no matter how sick I felt.

With an iron will, I steeled myself to open the door and tiptoe into the hall.

Col grabbed his things and followed.

We managed to make it downstairs without killing ourselves, but when Col opened the front door, he quickly closed it again and put a finger to his lips.

There was a sound of horses outside, lots of horses, and the shouts of many men.

"You're still here?" snapped the innkeeper's wife as she strode past us. "I sent Simon up to retrieve your tub an hour ago. But he must've left you to sleep in. Still, there's no room for you tonight." She glared at us as if we had done something wrong.

"Why not?" I asked.

The woman's face had gone pale. "The Harrow's soldiers are here. Almost half his army, seems like. They'll be needing a place to stay, some of them, as the barracks aren't big enough to hold all of them. Most of the inns in Prismvale will be taken up with them and their squires and servants."

I groaned, not only because we were being kicked

out, but because we had failed to find the thief before the soldiers arrived.

"Thank you," Col said.

He took my hand and led me to the back, where I imagined we would slide out a back door.

"And next time you come into town, don't bother coming here," the innkeeper's wife called after us. "I got complaints about all the racket last night. So you just be sure you find somewhere else."

Neither of us spoke as we let ourselves out the back, but my ears and face were burning with embarrassment. "What did we do?"

"No way of knowing now. I guess we'll just have to live with ourselves," Col said. I couldn't tell if he was being sarcastic or not. "We better get out of here," he said. "There's no sense in being caught by the soldiers now, after all this time."

We tiptoed through the back alleys of the city, stepping over human waste, rotten food, and very large rats, one of which bit my new boot when I accidentally put my foot down on its tail.

But we made it out of the city gates without anything worse happening. The sun was shining directly over us, and my head was pounding worse than ever. We hadn't eaten, and there was no chance of finding a potion to cure the hangovers. Part of me still wondered if I needed another kind of potion. I hadn't gotten my bleeding in months, something that often happened through the lean winter months and into spring. Whether it was from my siren heritage or my lack of food, I had never been able to figure out. Either way, I resolved to find ingredients for that potion as soon as possible. Just in case.

Col looked moody today. And broody. I frowned, wondering why those two words together made me want to giggle.

More soldiers passed us. They looked battle-worn and preoccupied, and didn't pay any attention to us.

"You really don't remember what happened?" I asked after we started down a side road, heading into farmland.

"I swear I don't know, Samara. Anyway," he said hurriedly, "we should probably figure out what we're doing today instead of what we did last night."

"Don't make it sound as if it's the worst thing that could happen to you, Col, man-who-sings-to-his-sword."

"I don't think anything of the sort," he said, turning. He reached up to tuck a loose strand of my hair behind my ear, and his voice softened. "Far from it. Let's find one of these little villages around the city. We can ask around, get some food, and decide our next move. We can talk then. I don't want to run into the soldiers, not when we're so outnumbered."

I only nodded—gently so as not to hurt my head—and followed, biting my lower lip, my skin burning where he'd brushed against it.

A short walk later, we were outside what looked like a poor village surrounded by farmland. Though the fields were bare this time of year, there were plenty of people about, and we found a small market stall that had some day-old bread and cheese. We bought it and went to sit on the other side of the stall to eat.

The seller didn't pay any attention as we ate, but he was busy packing up his things.

"Wonder where he's going?" I asked. "Hey! Something wrong?"

"I heard The Harrow's army is in Prismvale," he said crossly. "I don't want to be around when they get bored. It never ends well for the likes of us."

He glanced at Col's weapons, then shut his mouth tightly as if we had just lured him into saying something that would incriminate him. As soon as his wares were tucked into a small cart, he pulled them away from the village.

"Must be a general feeling," Col said. Several other people were rushing around, as if in a hurry to finish up business. "Guess that's our cue."

He stood and held out his hand for me, and I took it. With food, my headache had lessened, meaning there was no longer a pickaxe in my eye.

"If only we had a horse," I said.

"Look who's changed her tune."

I shot Col a glare, and we left the village. Before it was out of sight, we heard horses, and a brief glance back showed soldiers descending upon the buildings. Before long, they began entering them and dragging people out.

Col pulled me to the ground, and we hid in the brush beside the road.

"Are they searching for the thief or just having a little *fun*?" I asked, horrified for the villagers.

Col shook his head. "I don't want to stick around to find out," he said as he watched the soldiers. "Our best bet is to get back up into the mountains and hide. Much of this area has seen battle, and we might be able to find an abandoned place to regroup."

"But we have no idea what to do," I said. "We've lost the lead that we had on the soldiers, and it seems like they're still searching for the thief. And, if the thief is still around, they're likely to find them long before we do."

Col began leading me away from the road, into the cover of some trees, but I still saw the haunted look in his eyes. "It's my duty to keep searching, though."

"I wasn't suggesting we give up, but what do you mean by 'your duty'?"

"You should probably go home," he continued as if I hadn't asked anything. "Or I'll find a place for you to be safe until I return. Then I'll take you home myself."

"And just leave me here to hide from the soldiers? Not happening. Anyway, your arm isn't healed. How will you manage?" Something about that last bit bothered me, but I couldn't put my finger on what.

"I can make the tea myself. There's no point in putting you in further danger."

"Right, as if I won't be in danger if I stay behind," I said sarcastically. Had I another reason to regret the night before? Had I made such a big fool of myself that he didn't want anything more to do with me? "Col, look at me."

He had been marching resolutely away, and I grabbed his arm.

The look of pain on his face when he turned around was unexpected, to say the least. "You would be better off running as far from here as you could get," he said softly.

"Don't tell me what would be best for me."

He shook his head, and his eyes still carried that haunted look. "So far this quest has failed, and the truth is that I don't know what happens next. Only that I'm going toward danger, not away from it."

I crossed my arms in front of my chest. "In case you missed the events of the last few weeks, danger is everywhere. It doesn't matter if you hide from it or seek it out, it can't be avoided."

Col took a deep breath. "It's not just the danger, and I'm not trying to tell you what to do. I don't want you to feel obligated, to feel tied to me."

I frowned. "That's all?"

"Yes."

"So help me, Col, if you are lying—"

He growled, threw up his hands. "Come with me, then, if you want," he said, turning. "But I warned you."

His voice had turned gravelly, but that haunted look had left his eyes. It intrigued me. What was he hiding, and did I care? I wanted to believe he was telling the truth. Not only did I not want to be stranded in a strange place so near The Harrow's soldiers, but the thought of parting from Col made my insides do a funny flip. It was a slight, painful tug that was only relieved when he gave in.

Anyway, I had my own ideas for getting that alicorn horn, and Col wasn't going to talk me out of going. I hurried to catch up to him.

I scoffed. "The only reason I'm going is I don't think you can make the tea yourself," I said, knowing full well that he could.

Col swept his gaze along my face. "You did mention

it was poison if not brewed correctly," he answered, playing along.

"Yes," I said. "The ingredients, as you know, aren't that rare. It's just about knowing what to do."

An understanding passed between us, along with some of the heat from the night before.

"Guess you can't get rid of me so easily," I said smugly.

"Guess not."

We kept parallel to the road for most of the day, moving in and out of hiding as needed, down the valley and away from The Harrow's city, soldiers, and even lands, toward the border with Glimmerdale. I took some side trips along the way, to gather ingredients for Col's tea—which he only needed once a day now—and some extra for a tea of my own.

The countryside had more soldiers than I would have expected, and many of them looked battle worn and weary just as the others had, but either they didn't see us or were too preoccupied to notice.

"Where are they coming from?" I asked as we watched the third group pass our hiding place.

"There must have been a battle," said Col, his keen eyes taking in the soldiers' every detail.

Soon enough, we saw that he was right. Injured men began walking by, their armor, if they wore any, torn and dented and covered in blood. Behind them came others being drawn in wagons, not dead but moaning.

And then, as we went farther, we saw the dead, lying where they had fallen, and the ground began to grow soggy with the blood. The dead were Harrowfell and

Glimmerdale soldiers alike, but more of the latter. Many more. It was easy enough to tell the two armies apart with the elves' pointed ears and fine features. The Glimmerdale warriors wore light, elegant armor with the insignia of a scroll and quill. Many of them had tattoos on their faces. The Harrow's soldiers bore his symbol of a skull and vial, and their armor, though heavier, was not as finely made.

"It was a slaughter," I said, gaping at the bodies everywhere.

As we walked farther, we saw many more. Here, it looked as if The Harrow's soldiers had given as good as they had gotten, and the losses were even—that is, until I saw the first pyre of elven bodies burning in the fields. The stench was unimaginable, and I fought the urge to vomit for the second time that morning.

I wanted to turn and leave, to run up into the hills, into the safety of the mountains, anything to not walk through a fresh battlefield.

"The Harrow's soldiers caught up with Glimmerdale and started massacring them," Col said quietly.

"H-how can you tell that?"

He looked around at the bodies, at the fires, and the blood-soaked ground. "Their tracks. Glimmerdale elves don't shoe their horses, for one thing. But I have seen this sort of slaughter before."

I was too stunned to ask him when or why.

There were a few living among the dead, and some of them stopped their screaming long enough to beg for water. Col had a little in his water skin, and stopped when he saw them. The first man was a Harrowfell soldier, so beaten and bloody that his face was swollen like he had been swarmed by bees. When I saw the hole in his skull and the blood on the ground, I knew he didn't have long. It was a mystery how he'd managed to call for help.

Col lifted his head and held the water skin to his lips, but the man died before he tasted it, the water dribbling out of his mouth even as Col tried to help him.

I turned and retched then, losing my breakfast in the mud of the battlefield. My headache worsened, and all I could think of was getting away from the stench and the shock of so many mutilated bodies.

But Col found another man crying for help, and I passed him what little water I had. This time, I helped set the man in a sitting position while Col gave him something to drink.

The soldier drank, his face deathly white, but when he was done, he smiled, and blood ran out of his mouth. I force myself to watch and not to turn away like a coward.

"Such a waste," I said, "all so one man can become king of the world."

Col nodded as he eased the soldier back to the ground.

I realized that my hatred for The Harrow's soldiers, while not gone, had diminished. For the first time, I realized that no person in their right mind would come to a battlefield to die unless either they'd been lied to, or they didn't have a choice.

And while I knew there were warriors who celebrated dying on the battlefield as a way to achieve immortality, I realized, looking at these young, still-lanky men, that it wasn't the case here. Many of them were younger than me, not yet able to grow a beard, and they were dying for The Harrow.

When we ran out of water, Col still didn't stop finding the survivors. Not because he could do anything for them, but he said no one deserved to die alone.

Feeling helpless, exhausted, and ashamed of myself, I brushed away the tears on my cheeks and helped. I never strayed far from him, but kept within earshot as I walked the battlefield. My new boots were bloody, and I knew they would always carry the stink of this place. Many of the injured from Glimmerdale had been slaughtered where they lay, evidenced by the wounds speared into their backs, necks, and heads, leaving them so mangled that I avoided any elves from there on, if I could help it. None of them had been left alive, but I wondered at Harrowfell soldiers dying in pools of their own blood and shit, abandoned to die an agonizing death. Killing the wounded Glimmerdale elves had been more merciful.

Again, I lost what little was left in my stomach, but quickly wiped my mouth on my sleeve and kept up the work.

One soldier asked me to pray for him, but I could barely get the words out. "Find peace, and may the goddess welcome you with open arms, and her husband, the god of the Bitter Realms, provide a place for you to rest."

I didn't think I said the prayer correctly, but it must have been close enough because the soldier smiled and laid his head back with a final sigh.

It went on and on like that for the rest of afternoon

and into the evening. I'd stopped retching, when there was nothing left for me to throw up, and at some point, my hot tears of anger stopped as well. Instead, in my heart burned a renewed hatred for The Harrow, blazing through my chest and expanding into my limbs like a fire catching in a dry forest.

I hoped that someday, somehow, I would see The Harrow pay for his sins. And his Deviants, too. We saw evidence of their destructive death magic over great swaths of fields that were blackened and burned down to ash and bones.

When the sun had set and the air was turning brutally cold, Col found me to show me something—a medallion of some sort that had been torn off a leather strap. But I didn't know what it was.

"The Deviants of lower levels wear these," Col said.

He took me to where he'd found the medallion, around the neck of a man dressed in a hooded cloak, a broken mask hanging off his young face. He bore a crest that I had seen once before—a red serpent on a gold background. I shuddered. His hands had been burned to the bone.

"Spell went wrong," Col said.

I stared at the mage, but found no pity for him. He had died a suitable death, it seemed, parts of his robes burned away to reveal charred flesh beneath.

He opened his eyes, and I jumped back in shock.

His glazed eyes landed on me, and they burned with the same hatred for me as I felt for him. I never knew how the Deviants could sense my siren blood—even my slight greenish undertone usually went unnoticed—but they always did.

"Witch!" he said, and made a significant effort to spit on me. The spittle didn't make it past his lips, however, and he ended up drooling on himself.

"You will speak with a civil tongue," Col said with a growl. "Or I will make sure whatever pain you're experiencing now is nothing compared to what you will feel before you die."

I thought Col was bluffing, but when he grabbed the mage's burned stump and squeezed it, the mage wailed. When Col released his arm, the Deviant laid his head back and began to cry.

"I didn't know..." he said. "Didn't know."

He took a pained breath, and I saw the deep gash in his side that seemed to have gone septic. Blood was still leaking out of it, and it already smelled. It was a toss-up as to which of his injuries would kill him first—the burns or the wound.

"What did you not know?" I asked, though I had little desire for the answer.

"I didn't know what they had."

And then he closed his eyes and took two more breaths, each one weaker than the last.

"Where did they take it?" Col asked. He shook the Deviant's shoulders, and the mage opened his eyes and blinked up at Col, almost in surprise, as if he had forgotten we were there. "It is out of your reach now. It's on its way to The Harrow, and..." He gulped down a ragged breath. "And the elven thieves have been punished."

The Deviant looked into Col's eyes and began to laugh. More blood bubbled out of him, out of his mouth, his nose, and even his eyeballs. It oozed out of his chest faster, and yet he still laughed, the echo of it bouncing over the battlefield.

Revulsion turned my stomach.

The mage was still laughing when he saw Col's raven ring, and his eyes widened. Then the laughing stopped abruptly, and all the breath seemed to whisper out of him. He was dead.

Col didn't speak words over this one, and neither did I. The mages didn't believe in the old gods anyway, preferring to revere the mysterious new gods who supposedly gave them their powers.

When Col stood, he wiped his hands on his clothes as if disgusted. "What do you make of that?"

"I... It sounds like he knew what we were after. But how?"

"The Deviants can't read minds, nor can they tell the future, although they would like us to believe they can. But they have other ways of seeing people. Perhaps he sensed it."

"He was looking for the alicorn horn."

Col nodded. "And if he is right, if he wasn't lying, which I don't think he was, then the alicorn horn has been found. And it is far out of our reach now."

Col sat back on his heels and cursed under his breath.

I preferred to curse openly. "Fuck." There was no hope for getting the horn now. "What is that insignia?" I asked. "I've seen it before... on the Deviants who captured me."

"It is Moredanea's crest."

"Who's Moredanea?"

"The Harrow's pet, as she's sometimes called. She's a powerful mage who practically never leaves his side. And she does much of his dirty work for him. Whatever horrors you have heard about The Harrow, many of them were perpetrated by Moredanea. In some ways, she is viler than him." Finally, he stood. "Let's get out of this wretched place."

We were almost at the end of the battlefield, which had stretched on for what seemed an eternity in every direction. But there was an end to it, and though Col stopped a couple more times, most of the people on this end were already dead.

"This must have been the front lines," he said.

We came to a wooded area and encountered a crowd of people. Peasants, soldiers, children even. They had all gathered around a tall tree, one that stood straight and towered over any of the others in the area. Its bark was blackened as if damaged by fire, its leaves as black as midnight. And the people around it were standing with their hands clasped, or kneeling on the ground, or even kissing it while they wept. There were live soldiers removing their armor.

"I've heard about this," I said. "The tree is rare. And though it looks like it's been burned, that's how it grows."

Col nodded. "Some believe the tree will transfer prayers up to the heavens, to any gods who might be listening. And that the tree itself can provide healing."

Col's voice had grown grim, and I followed his gaze to several dead soldiers lying within a few feet of the tree, as if they had crawled there to ask for healing, and had died.

"I suppose the tree can do just as much as the gods," I said scornfully.

Col laughed humorlessly. "The gods... who cares if they are real, because if they are, they don't care one bit about our prayers. They play with us until it suits them, and when they're done, they stomp on us like a child stomps on an anthill."

I felt the bitterness in his words, rolling off his body in waves, and I couldn't disagree.

We left the battlefield behind us, hoping to find shelter for the night. We had passed burned homes and even one abandoned village, but we weren't about to go back through the battlefield to get to them. That way lay only death.

There were a few villages around, small, poor ones that sprang up after the battles. The peasants had nowhere to go, so they kept replanting ruined crops, kept building temporary homes, and kept hiding from the armies.

Col passed the first village completely, saying it smelled wrong to him. I was too tired to argue even though I wanted nothing more than to sleep. Yet I was afraid of stopping, too troubled by what I had seen, knowing the images would be there in my mind when I closed my eyes.

Eventually, we came to a house that was slightly bigger than some of the others, with a large barn behind it. Col spoke to the elderly farmer who came to the door, who let us pay him to stay in his barn for the evening. He even spared some goat's milk, along with some nuts and bread.

The barn was large enough for horses, but instead only housed goats. They bleated as we walked in, but otherwise went back to munching on their hay. There was a loft above them, and we climbed the ladder, spreading Col's cloak over the hay to make it more comfortable.

"There's a well right behind the barn," Col said, climbing down the ladder again. He returned quickly, lugging an entire bucket of water and some cloths. "The farmer gave me these," he said.

I dipped one of the cloths in the bucket and began to wipe it over my face and neck. The day had been a dirty one, and I couldn't imagine what I looked like. "The bath is all gone," I said with a half-smile.

"Here," Col said, holding out his hand for the rag. I gave it to him, and he began to wipe the side of my cheek. "Missed a spot."

I closed my eyes and enjoyed the sensation of being taken care of. No one had taken care of me since my mother died, not even my father, who had been so absorbed in his own grief that he had forgotten me and Laney. Flint would have helped, but he was gone. Col had been trying to take care of me for some time now, and I had been blind to it.

I sobbed, unable to stifle the sharp pain that pierced my chest.

Col removed the rag from where he'd been cleaning my neck. "Did I hurt you? Are you injured?"

I shook my head and wiped the tears on my face.

Then I remembered my hands were dirty and sighed. Col rinsed out the rag and then began to clean my hands. His strokes were sure, firm but gentle. When my hands were clean, he wiped the new smudges on my face. "There, my little siren, all clean."

I noted he had called me a siren this time, and not a songbird, and wondered why.

His hand lingered on my face, and he dropped the rag. There was nothing between us, then, and for some reason, I felt naked under his gaze, with nothing to stop him from seeing who I really was. How bare and helpless I felt at that moment. How utterly wretched and power-less and small.

And suddenly, I realized that I hadn't torn down the wall protecting my heart against this mysterious, high-born man.

It had simply crumbled somewhere along the way. And as the wall had disintegrated, Col's warmth was melting the ice behind it.

CHAPTER SIXTEEN

*C*ol didn't ask why I was crying, why hot tears were streaking down my face and onto his hand. He didn't back away, repulsed by my display of emotion.

Instead, he leaned in and kissed the tears away. He brushed his lips over each cheek, turning my head with a hand on my chin. I thought he would do more, but he sat back and gave me a sad smile. His hand moved to my shoulder, holding me in place, tethering me to him, anchoring me.

I couldn't stand it anymore. His gaze pierced my soul, and he saw me... yet he didn't run away. I didn't know if I could handle it. "You'd think I'd have learned my lesson, after that monumental hangover this morning," I said to lighten the moment, to make him forget my tears, "but I wish we had more of that goblin whiskey."

"Why?" he asked.

I shuddered and decided to be honest. "To forget today, maybe. To distract myself, to maybe go to sleep and not hear the dying beg for water and prayers."

Col took a long, shuddering breath. His hand left my shoulder in favor of running down my arm, and my skin prickled beneath my clothes. "I don't have any goblin whiskey, Samara, but would you take me as a substitute?"

My breath hitched in my throat, and I took a moment to process what he just said. I wanted to think I understood, but I also wanted to make sure my ears weren't deceiving me.

As if he knew my struggle and didn't want to create confusion, Col leaned forward to kiss me on the lips, slowly and languidly, as if there was no rush, no world outside this barn.

I moaned, opening my mouth for his tongue, wrapping my arms around his neck, trying to get as close to him as possible. His hands slid to my waist and wrapped around me, pulling me in.

After a moment, I pulled back, breathing heavily. "You are a better substitute, I think."

"You 'think'?" he growled. "Maybe I better give you another taste."

And then his lips swept against mine, and before I knew it he had me straddling him, his hands on my hips and sweeping down my backside to rub me against him, to show me just how hard he was for me.

He was very, very hard.

And I melted completely. All thoughts but those of him had already abandoned my mind, leaving my body free to take over. I ground my hips against him, yearning to feel that enormous cock against my most sensitive areas, earning myself a wicked bite on the lip before Col made his way down to kiss my neck.

We fell back onto the cloak, my legs wrapped around Col's waist, refusing to break contact even though I wanted more more *more*. He kissed me again, slowing down to explore my mouth with his tongue, tasting me, lapping my lips seductively as if his tongue were somewhere else on my body. Then he slowed down to look at me again.

"Do you really want this?" he asked. He stilled his hand, which had been making its way down to my hip. I wriggled beneath him, pushing my hips up into his.

"So much," I said, afraid of how true it was.

He shuddered, and his eyes darkened and then glowed like coals, as if he was releasing something within himself. After another moment of hesitation, he said, "Gods, Samara, I want you too."

Yes. My heart said it just before my lips did, and then he was crashing his mouth to mine, rolling his hips into me while his hands began to roam once again.

I felt strange with this man. Like he had opened up my heart and thawed it, removing the barriers around it, and at the same time, had taught me to be stronger. How had he weakened and strengthened me in the same breath?

I wrapped my legs around him, urging his hips into mine, seeking a release from the pressure that was already too much to bear. Frantically, I began unbuttoning his shirt, shoving my hands onto his chest, desperate to have his skin pressed to mine.

But he slowed my hands, pulling off me just a little, his hips still slowly moving in circles.

"Please," I groaned. "Please."

I had never begged before, but something about it only made me more eager for him.

Col let go of my hands and then sat up on his knees between my legs, and began to undo his shirt, slowly and with his eyes fixed on me. I sat up then, doing the same. I didn't want to wait any longer for our clothes to be removed, nor did I want to let him drag it out. I wanted to see that gorgeous body, wanted to feel those muscles drag against my breasts as he fucked me.

Oh gods I was horny.

My shirt came off the same time his did; I pulled off my thin camisole as well. There was just enough light to see him gaze at my breasts with hunger in his eyes. They weren't very big, and they didn't compare at all to that serving girl's, the one who wanted to sell more ale.

"Perfect," he said, dispelling my moment of insecurity. "I've never seen anyone shaped so exquisitely as you."

I scoffed. "Now that's got to be a lie, Col."

He shook his head. "I would never lie to you, Samara," he said quietly. A muscle twitched in his jaw, but then he seemed to let go of whatever troubled him and palmed my breasts.

Still sitting between my legs, he flicked a thumb over my right nipple, which was already peaked and conscious of the man in front of me.

I gasped and leaned into him, closing my eyes. He took my left breast in his mouth, and the sensation of his lips on my nipple, his tongue flicking back and forth, made me want to just tear the rest of my clothes off and tackle him.

But he seemed to enjoy teasing me, holding me still as he gave each nipple his full attention. I began to breathe raggedly. I still half straddled him in a ridiculous position, so I leaned back on my elbows. He followed, and then he began deliberately rolling his hips into mine once again. The sensation was exquisite, and yet definitely not enough.

I reached between us to try to free that present waiting in his pants, but he grabbed my wrist and pushed my hand above my head. "Not yet, my love," he growled.

My love. He'd used the phrase before, almost as a pet name, but tonight it shot tingles straight to my core, as if my body wanted nothing more than to hear that word on his lips again.

He was still attending to my breasts, alternating between them, kneading and sucking. I was so frustrated I wanted to scream, and pushed my hips up into his, trying to hurry things along.

Col chuckled against my nipple and then dragged it between his teeth.

"Oh!" I said, hissing and freeing his hair. I weaved my fingers through it, enjoying the sensation. His hair was soft and thick, luxurious even, and I was glad he kept it long. He caught my other nipple between his teeth, and I tugged his hair in response.

"Impatient, siren?"

"You know I am," I gasped.

I felt helpless beneath Col, but he didn't hurry along for my sake. Instead, he pinned my arm above my head and went back to sucking on my nipple, occasionally using his teeth to send what felt like sparks straight to my core.

I still had one hand free, and this time I tried to undo his pants. But to my dismay, he grabbed that hand too. "My arm is feeling much better this evening," he said mischievously. He placed my right hand with the left and held them with one of his own, pressing me into the hay.

"Is this what's meant by having a roll in the hay?" I asked, wriggling deliciously beneath him. Col laughed, and the sensation of his bare chest against mine nearly ended me. "I want more of you, Col, *all* of you. Now."

"As you wish, my lady," he said quietly, placing a kiss on my mouth. He then disentangled himself from me and began removing his pants. I quickly removed mine, shedding my undershorts at the same time. He had already seen me naked, and I was ready to do more than just look at each other. I didn't care if we took down the barn around us, I just needed to feel him inside me.

"Col," I said, reaching for him. Finally, he let me touch his hard cock. It was bigger than any I'd seen before, though I was no expert, and I practically moaned when I thought about what it would feel like inside me. I stroked him, letting my fingertips run over the tip, flicking my thumb into his slit, just like I wanted to do with my tongue.

Speaking of... I leaned forward, my mouth open, leaving no doubt about where I was heading, but Col groaned and grabbed my chin, made me look at him. His eyes were dark and blazing at the same time.

He shook his head. "I don't think I can handle that tonight, my little siren." And with a wicked grin, he began to kiss me again. His lips were slow, languorous, and yet I could taste his urgency as much as I could feel my own. I grabbed his length again, this time running my hands down the shaft before finding his balls and giving them a gentle squeeze.

He laughed and groaned at the same time, his tongue forcing its way into my mouth, as if he wanted to live there. I began to stroke him, lightly at first, and then exploring. Finding his most sensitive spots. Col moaned. Breathing roughly, he stopped kissing me and put his forehead on my shoulder.

And I felt powerful. Seductive. Trusted.

He took my wrist, and after encouraging me to stroke him a couple of times, stilled my hand, gripping it hard. When he opened his eyes, I was smiling just like he had, wickedly and without mercy.

Removing my hand from his cock altogether, he pushed me backward and began to kiss along my jaw, his lips then trailing down my neck to my collarbone. He skipped my now-tender breasts, and the rough scrape of his short beard moved down my belly.

I hoped he was headed farther down, but then I felt the sharp tip of a blade on my skin, and gasped.

Col's eyes were molten as he watched me, my dagger —his old one—unsheathed and tracing an invisible line on my ribs. It tickled, but I didn't dare move. The tip of that blade was incredibly sharp, and only his skillful hands kept it from opening a wound on my skin.

"You wanted to know about my kinks," he said mischievously.

I swallowed, mesmerized by the dagger's path up my

ribcage and to my breast. The tip paused delicately on the peak of my nipple, and I trembled. Not because I didn't trust Col, but because he knew I trusted him, and wanted me to prove it.

The blade passed over my nipple and then moved up over my collarbone. Gently, dangerously, he placed it under my chin and lifted it so that I looked him in the eye.

"Don't fucking move," he commanded. I felt that euphoric bliss settle over me, and a voice in my head told me to obey.

Whether he was using his compulsion magic on me or not, I had every reason to do as I was told, so I held his gaze as the dagger traced a path between my breasts, over my belly, and to my sex. Leaving a trail of goosebumps on my skin that made my breath hitch in my throat. When the dagger barely whispered over my clit, I moaned, wanting more than anything to deepen the pleasure but knowing that to move would be disastrous.

The torture intensified when he ran a finger through my folds, the dagger positioned so that I was forced to hold still, and I bit down on my lip to keep from crying out as he deftly inserted his finger and began to stroke me. I whimpered then, wanting to cry and yelp at the same time because it was so delicious, but knowing that under no circumstances should I make any sudden movements.

When he inserted a second finger, and then a third, I shattered around them. It was so sudden that my surprise made me open my mouth in a silent scream, but I managed to keep the rest of my body still. Except for the part of me that was spasming around his fingers.

"That won't do, my little siren," Col said, his voice thick with desire. "I want to hear you come. I demand it."

I took a ragged breath. "I hate you right now."

"No you don't."

He tossed the dagger aside, and I almost groaned in disappointment. Pushing my legs farther apart, he settled between them with a kiss to my inner thigh.

"Oh sweet gods," he said. "You smell so good."

Col swept a finger along my sex, skimming over the area I most wanted him to touch. When that finger slipped just inside me again, I groaned at the same time he did.

"So wet," he breathed, letting the air tickle me, making me squirm. "I've wanted to taste this pussy for a long time, ever since you rode behind me on that horse..."

When his lips found my tender center, I cried out. My body was now free, and I threaded my fingers through his hair once again, urging him on. "Col!"

He paused long enough to say, "Say my name like that again, love."

"Col," I said, pleading with him to continue.

He shifted position a little and then placed his tongue on me again. He flicked it over my lower lips and then thrust it inside me, and fire pooled in my belly.

Then he replaced his tongue with two fingers, not easing into me like before, but slipping them inside me together in one swift motion.

I almost came undone right there.

And then his lips and tongue found my clit, and he

began to devour me. I was breathing quickly in no time, my legs wrapped around his shoulders, writhing beneath him with my hands threaded through his hair. When I nearly bucked him off, he chuckled and held my hips down with one strong arm while his fingers worked their magic, finding a spot I didn't know existed and bringing me to the brink.

It felt good to let go, to simply feel something other than pain or sorrow or anger. I associated none of those things with Col.

I was breathing raggedly now, and when he hit that spot inside me and pressed it, I split around him. My mind and body shattered as pleasure wreaked havoc on my body for the second time. My hips bucked off the blanket, and he pushed them back down, continuing his torture. I cried out, then, unable to even say his name because I was so undone.

He didn't let up, and a few seconds later another wave of pleasure built so fast that I didn't even have time to realize what was happening before my body shuddered and my mouth opened in another silent cry.

He clamped his hands on my hips, held me still, and continued to eat me like I was a feast at the king's castle.

The pleasure intensified, and I screamed, this time managing to get his name in there too. "Col!"

A goat made a grunting noise below us, and I laughed, even as I continued to ride this latest wave of pleasure that was sweeping over my body.

Col finally stilled, and I sank back to catch my breath. He removed his fingers and then spread my lower lips, as if he were trying to peer directly inside me. I was suddenly self-conscious even though he had just had his mouth and tongue all over me.

When Col replaced his gaze with his tongue, I yelped. I was so sensitive, and already responding to him again. Without warning, he shoved his tongue all the way inside me, tasting me before finally, finally withdrawing and kissing his way back up my belly.

"Kiss me," he demanded when he looked me in the eye.

I did, and I tasted myself on him. It wasn't something I particularly enjoyed, but the way he demanded it, and the way he had devoured me, was opening my senses to a new world of possibilities, and I found I liked it. Maybe it was my scent mixed with *him* that made it so erotic, so welcome.

When Col drew away, I must have whimpered.

"Don't worry, Samara. We're just getting started."

Then he took himself in hand and began to rub the head of his cock along my slick folds. It felt so good, that soft velvety head on the very brink, so close to where I wanted it and yet too far. He looked into my eyes, and I smiled.

"All of you," I reiterated. I wasn't about to let him stop now, even though I didn't think he needed any urging.

Col entered me slowly, his cock warm and slick. I felt the way it stretched me, enjoyed the sensation of him burying himself to the hilt inside me. I even felt when his balls touched my folds, adding to the pleasure. "Col..." I moaned.

"How do you like my sword now?" he asked with a teasing smile.

I laughed and wriggled my hips, driving myself against him, and he bent to kiss me again. And then, even as our lips were locked, he began thrusting in and out of me, slowly but firmly, burying himself in me each time. Each slide of his cock against my flesh was delicious, each movement controlled and yet with a hint that just beyond was uncontrollable passion. Col rolled his hips a little, listening and feeling for when I would gasp or moan. And then he would keep doing whatever he had done so that I would moan and gasp some more, and I felt cherished.

"You are incredible, Samara," he said. The intensity of his gaze took my breath away, and as if to keep me with him, he held my chin. "Incredible," he repeated.

We began a time of discovery. I moved my hips in time with him, searching for that beautiful tandem, that build of aching pleasure. Col did the same, and each stroke of his body against mine was like the opposite of torture—whatever that was.

This. This was the opposite of torture, and yet felt so torturous anyway.

I gasped as he began to increase his pace, and my nails dug into his back, urging him on. "Col."

"Samara," he whispered.

With one more thrust, I came undone for the fourth time that night, this time screaming his name and clutching him to me, trying to keep him as deep inside me as he could go. Col was panting, and he thrust inside me once. Twice. Three more times, and then he made a sound that was somewhere between a groan and cry. His body shuddered against me over and over again.

As he finished, he kissed me, and I felt utterly taken, and also greedy, because I knew already that I wanted more of him.

Col pulled slowly out and sank down beside me. His cock, still hard, rested on my thigh.

I touched his face, trying to decipher the lines around his eyes, in one so young, and whatever burden was troubling him, wishing it away. He deserved good things. Great things. And I hoped someday I saw him come into his own, whatever that might be.

I knew right then and there I wanted to spend more time with this man, that the thought of leaving him caused a lump in my throat. I didn't want to think about what that meant, however. Not yet.

Col's fingers moved languidly over my stomach, occasionally running up and flicking a nipple. I lay there in the moonlight and let him play with my body, enjoying the sensations, trying to keep from squirming, making it a game. But when his fingers rolled over my ribs, I twitched and grabbed his hand.

"That's enough now. We don't want your shoulder to have a setback," I said with a wide grin.

"Samara, you are the best kind of medicine I could have right now."

I rolled onto my stomach, placing a kiss on the raven tattoo on his chest. Col rubbed his calloused hand over my backside and squeezed it. "This beautiful ass," he said admiringly. "Do you forgive me?"

I took his nipple between my teeth and gently pulled on it before saying, "Depends on what happens next."

Col smacked my ass playfully, and I yelped. He began massaging away the sting, but I took his nipple again and bit hard, until he hissed. He sat up, bringing me with him, and grabbed my chin, his other hand still kneading my ass. I straddled him and pushed him back so I could be on top. This time, I was going to be in control.

"If you're good," I said, "someday I might let you do that again with your sword."

Col grabbed my hips and gave them a squeeze. "I knew you liked it," he said with a smirk.

I gave him a poke in the ribs and leaned over him. "Asshole."

Much later, when we finally landed in a heap on the now rumpled cloak, I pulled hay out of my mouth and laughed. It was in my hair and his. After we'd straightened the cloak and picked off most of the hay, we lay beside each other, my head on his chest, one of my legs thrown across his thigh. We were sweaty and sticky and utterly sated. I had never felt so complete in my life, and sighed contentedly.

"You never told me how you like my sword," Col said seriously.

I raised my head to look at him. "I'm pretty sure I did."

"No, you never said it."

I gave him a peck on the cheek. "I thought it was well made," I said with a grin. "Well-formed. Congratulations to your parents."

Col began tickling me then, and I shrieked, trying to

get on top of him, to hold him down, but he was much too strong for me; he flipped us over and once again pinned my arms above my head.

"And my tongue?" he asked before kissing me deeply.

When he raised up to let me speak, I was out of breath again. "Masterful," I said, knowing exactly what I was telling him.

"That's more like it." He kissed me again, and then, though we couldn't seem to get enough of touching each other, we fell asleep in each other's arms. And I didn't remember the last time I had been so content.

CHAPTER SEVENTEEN

I woke to a strange sound. Col was gone, and for a moment I struggled to remember where I was. The noise came again—grunting not unlike that of pigs, and yet a bit more otherworldly. "Col," I hissed. When he didn't respond, I hurried to get dressed. Grabbing my sword, I climbed down the ladder. Something had disturbed the goats, and they were bleating and moving around restlessly.

"I've been killing these fuckers all day," a strange voice said. A stranger was standing outside the barn. "They've been breeding in the great battlefield, feeding on the dead and dying."

I ran outside, only to see Col standing between the barn and the house with another man. An enormous man with a great ax. He spun the ax a few times, warming up, while Col approached the gap between the farmer's house and the barn. There, in the shadows of the moon, I saw something move. It was big, at least half the height of the barn itself.

"Shit," Col said.

"Yeah," the other man agreed.

Towering over them was a hairy monster with rows of needle-sharp teeth that reminded me of a possum's, except much bigger.

The man with the ax caught up with Col and charged the monster, his ax sinking straight into the creature's side. It shrieked and pivoted, and the new man let out a steady stream of curses as he followed. The monster moved into the moonlight, and I saw fur around its neck and ears like that of a mouse, claws on all four feet, and a leather-like hide that was now gleaming with blood.

I took it all in for a split second before Col swept his sword toward the creature, which was already dodging the other man. Its tail was covered in spikes that dug into the ground and propelled it away from them.

Col and the big man followed, attacking. Col's sword gleamed in the moonlight and then sliced through the armor as if it were paper. The creature screeched, and then hissed at him, its tail lashing out like a dangerous whip. He ducked, and the other man attacked from the side, driving it backward with his ax, its runes glowing just like Col's sword.

Together, they backed the monster into a corner against the barn, making enough racket to wake people for miles around.

They were just preparing two killing blows to its head when I heard something else.

"Col!" I yelled in warning. Col glanced to me. "There's another one!"

"Samara, run!" he yelled.

The second monster had seen me, too, and its eyes almost seemed to glow with rage... or hunger. The giant rodent lunged for me just as Col plunged his sword into the side of the first one. I turned and ran around the corner of the barn, looking for cover. Behind me, Col called my name. A candle appeared in the window of the farmer's house, but I veered away from it. The last thing I wanted was for the monster to attack the people who had given us shelter.

I could feel it behind me. I wasn't going to outrun it. Halfway across the field, I stopped and spun around, my sword drawn.

This second monster was at least twice the size of the first, and its eyes really did glow, and it had wings.

I shouted for Col and took a few steps back. The second beast was flapping into the air, snapping its jaws at my outstretched sword.

Then Col was there, grabbing me around the waist and pushing me behind him. The other man appeared at his side, the runes in his ax so bright that they threatened to destroy my night vision.

Col told me to go back to the barn, but I was in awe of this thing, and the men who stood between me and it.

"Samara! Did you hear me?"

"Yes, I damn well heard you, but if you think I'm going to run away while you get eaten by that... that thing, then you haven't been paying attention."

Despite the urgency of the situation, Col laughed. "Don't let that thing's tail get too close!"

The other man had already engaged the monster, drawing it away from us, and Col ran to join him.

The big man was holding his own. He had damaged the beast already, and, ducking to avoid its tail, Col dove toward it with a mighty roar. He thrust his blade into the animal's neck, and blood ran down his arms. The other man aimed for the head, and together, they finished it off.

The first pale rays of light were shining in the far east, outlining a silhouette of the mountains.

"What the hell is that thing?" I asked as Col cleaned his sword in the grass.

"A ghoul rat," the new man said. "A hybrid vermin. A nasty, venomous rat that lays its eggs in corpses for the young to eat when they hatch, like a fly."

"Samara and I didn't see any yesterday when we walked through the battlefield," Col said.

"They had probably already laid their eggs and left. This one," the stranger said, kicking the dead monster, "is the adult version. The other was newly hatched."

"*Newly hatched?*" I asked.

The other man's eyes swept over me in an assessing way, and he nodded. "They grow really fast at first, especially if there's been a big battle. The more corpses they eat... Well, you can imagine."

I stared down at the creature with a look of disgust.

"I knew you had someone with you, Col," said the newcomer, "but I was one step behind, and I kept getting stopped by these damn monsters. If I take their heads to Prismvale, I could probably get a few coins from the magistrate for them."

"Oh?" Col asked. "Does he pay monster hunters?"

"That cowardly fucker? Not exactly. The bastard wants people to think he killed them. He'll have them dried and prepared, and hang them in his manor. Hell, for all I know, he jerks off to them."

"Sounds like he's overcompensating," I said.

Both men laughed, and Col put his arm around my waist, drawing me to him. "Samara, this is one of my oldest friends, Magnus."

"You have friends?" I asked with a smirk.

Magnus bowed slightly. "My lady."

I shifted on me feet. "I'm not a lady."

"Col would only be in the company of ladies," he said, glancing at Col with a cheeky grin.

"That's enough, Magnus," Col said. "Anyway, didn't you have something to tell me?"

"Yes," Magnus said. He was the largest man I had ever seen. Tall, muscular, covered in scars and tattoos. "Would the lady give me a moment with my friend?" His gaze turned on me and then darted back to Col.

I don't know why I expected Col to say something like, "You can say anything in front of her," but he didn't.

Instead, he nodded, and I was surprised. I had no right to expect to hear a private conversation, and no right to demand that Col not keep secrets from me, but it disappointed me, anyway. And I was suddenly curious, too.

"Samara?" Col asked, his gaze searching mine.

I smiled at Magnus and said, "I'd rather stay out here, if you don't mind. If there are any more of those things lurking around, I'd rather be with the people who can kill them."

That part was true. The larger one had almost made

me faint when I'd spotted it. I also didn't like being dismissed like a child or a servant.

Col was looking at me strangely. It wasn't unkind, but it was intense. More intense than when I'd watched his face only a short time ago as he unleashed himself on my body. "Yes?" I asked.

Col glanced at Magnus and then sighed, running his hand through his hair, finding hay in it, and cursing lightly under his breath.

I hadn't thought hay in his hair would have been that big a deal, but it caused him to glare at Magnus and then at me. "She doesn't know, Magnus."

"Does she need to know?" the big man asked.

Col's gaze was searching my face. "Yes."

"Damn," Magnus said. He saw the hay, then looked at me. Finally, with a look of understanding, he clapped Col on the shoulder and stepped away. If Magnus had done that to me, I would have sprawled face down in the dirt, but I ignored him and looked at Col.

"Need to know what?" I asked.

Col cleared his throat. Behind him, Magnus called, "Just rip off that bandage."

Col chuckled but then took my hand. "What if I told you there's a big reason for me chasing down an alicorn horn."

I shrugged. "I'd say that wouldn't surprise me, not with the way you've been about it." I was becoming anxious, wondering what Col couldn't say but needed to, apparently. I'd known he was keeping something from me, and it seemed I was about to find out what it was.

We were all saved from the awkward moment when the farmer came out of his house and called to us.

Col sighed.

"Hello," said the farmer when he reached us. Though this wasn't the man Col had spoken to the night before. This one was at least twenty years younger.

"My father sent me to thank you," the young farmer said. "We woke up in time to hear the battle, and then he went outside to see the first monster that you killed. I'm glad you were here because I wouldn't have been able fight them off on my own. Not with just my pitchfork."

Magnus nodded. "I've been hunting these pieces of shit for days. You're lucky they hadn't appeared on your farm before now."

"We are fortunate, indeed. Please, come in and sit by the fire, and eat. It's the least I can do."

We accepted the farmer's hospitality and followed him to the house. The idea of a hot fire and food sounded good. Col glanced at me, and I stepped in closer to him as we walked. "What's the matter? Really?"

"It's only that I have something important to tell you," Col said quietly. "And... Maybe it would be better after we've eaten."

"Col, you're making me nervous. Just tell me already."

He sighed heavily and stopped walking. Magnus pretended like he hadn't seen and walked straight ahead with the farmer.

Col waited until they were out of earshot. Then, he put his hands on my shoulders and ran them down my arms to hold my hands. I let go of his hands and instead placed mine over his heart. "Unless you are going to tell me you are The Harrow himself, I don't care."

Col huffed a laugh. "I am most definitely not The Harrow. But The Harrow does play a big part in my story, one that I haven't told you much about."

I nodded for him to continue.

"My name is Col, as you know, but it's a nickname, not my full one. My real name is Andris, Prince and Heir to the throne of Iron Deep."

I blinked, trying to let what he'd said to sink in, and my mouth went dry. "Iron Deep." *From the North*, he'd told me more than once, but Iron Deep was far to the north, near the Dragon Lands. "But... Iron Deep fell to Harrowfell years ago."

Col's hands tightened on mine. "Several years ago, when I was only twelve, The Harrow invaded Iron Deep. My father summoned everyone he could to his banner, and it was the largest force Iron Deep had ever seen. But we were still no match for the size of The Harrow's army. Because I was young, my mother wanted to send me away.

"My father, the king, refused, saying my place was with my people, and that I was old enough to see war." Col's voice grew soft. "On the eve of what was to be a great battle, The Harrow sent assassins into my parents' tower. They had found a way in through their spies, and to this day I think someone in my father's inner circle betrayed him. Otherwise they would never have gotten in. My mother was killed in her sleep, her throat slit and her body... abused. My father was taken captive, even as his personal guard was slain. Other guards, once they saw what was happening, betrayed my father and let The Harrow's soldiers in.

"During the chaos of the fighting, my father's chamberlain found me. He somehow had my father's sword, which he handed to me, along with a pack of supplies. Then, he sent me off with my best friend, Kiaran, sneaking us out a secret way. I knew where to go, having explored the tunnels when I was younger. My friend and I escaped and met up with others, people who were already my allies even though I didn't realize it at the time. I was hunted for a long time. The Harrow was furious that I had escaped, but my friends kept me safe."

I was staring at him now, my mouth open in shock.

"Ever since," Col continued, "I have been in exile. I can't go back to my own kingdom, not without sufficient forces or help. My father was used as a puppet for many years. I think my mother's death broke him. And I think he believed I was dead, as well. But he eventually died, and his power was transferred to me. The Harrow's hold on Iron Deep is still strong, too strong, and he would do anything he could to catch me, to use me as he did my father."

I took a deep breath as everything clicked into place. "And you never told me because...?"

"As you can probably imagine, it's not wise to walk around using my real name. In fact, only Magnus and a few other close friends know my real identity—and now you. But I couldn't tell you in the beginning. I didn't know you."

I remembered all the flirtations, about sleeping together in the cold, huddled under the cloak. About the tavern and the bath... About last night. I had known he was holding something back, had known in my gut that he wasn't like me, that he wasn't *for* me.

And my heart cracked, threatening to break apart.

"Would *you* have said anything," he asked, "if the roles were reversed?"

I pulled away from him, shivering in the cold. "You said you would never lie to me," I said. I couldn't even look at him. The pressure on my chest felt like someone was standing on it, and I had to take a step back to get some air.

"I didn't lie to you, not directly. I only kept the truth from you because at first it didn't matter, and then later, I just wanted to find the right time."

"Was it all a ruse?" I asked, the anger building. "So you could fuck me and brag about the siren who let you between her legs?"

"No! Not at all. Everything I said about you is true. I care for you. I love you."

My heart, as if it had been lying under the weight of the mountain, burst. I couldn't accept his love. What was love to this man? He had been raised so differently from me. I had dared to think we were similar, he and I. But we were nothing alike, and everything I had imagined about his past was wrong.

"Samara?" Col asked.

But that wasn't his name, was it? It was Andris. Prince Andris of Iron Deep. He could never be with someone like me, not if he wanted his kingdom back. And he might have loved me, like he said, but when I looked into his eyes through my tears, I couldn't help feeling used and manipulated.

He took a step toward me, but I stepped back and held up my hand to stop him. "How long have you been able to use your arm?" I'd remembered flashes of him using it the night we got drunk together—had it only been two nights ago? And he'd fought that monster tonight as if there had never been anything wrong with his shoulder.

"A few days," Col said cautiously. "Its strength has returned off and on, that is, because as you know I struggled in the mountains. Samara, you saved my life."

"And that means that you get to fuck me? Or perhaps have some misguided affection for me?"

Col grabbed my arms. "Look at me, please. Please." I did, fixing him with my best glare. "Please don't walk away from me, Samara. My love for you is genuine, and it's not because you saved my life, though I'm grateful you did. Please don't walk away."

I pulled out of his reach, the tears flowing freely down my cheeks. The thought of parting with him was already tearing me apart, but it didn't stop me from saying, "I need to think about it."

Then I turned and walked to the farmer's house, refusing to look back. When I stepped inside, the warmth of the house and the large cheery fire in the hearth was almost insulting. Magnus eyed me warily, but I didn't speak to him as I accepted a cup of hot tea from the farmer's son. I thanked him and then sat in a chair in the corner of the room.

"You all right, lady?" the farmer's son asked.

I wiped my cheeks. "I will be," was all I said angrily.

Col entered then, but I refused to look at him, instead gazing into the fire and letting it dry my tears. Col accepted some tea and sat on a small bench near Magnus. The monster hunter looked back and forth between us but didn't say anything.

The farmers soon brought out a couple of platters of meat, cheese, bread, and goat's milk. They tried to open a bottle of ale as well, but I declined, and I noticed Col did too. Magnus, however, had no compunctions about drinking.

I ate a little, only picking at my food. It just didn't seem appetizing, though I tried because I didn't want to offend the farmer, who had been so kind. He asked Magnus several questions about the removal of the monsters, and the two of them seemed to come to some kind of agreement. They shook hands, but I really didn't care what happened to the carcasses. I was still rolling over everything in my mind about Col. *I love you*, he'd said. But what happened when he came to his senses and realized that I was just a thief? More than that, a half-breed thief?

And did I love him back? I wasn't sure.

"Why were you after the package?" I asked, suddenly looking at Col.

"Because I didn't want it used against another kingdom," he said. But he didn't offer anything else right then, and I knew he was thinking of the farmers. After a while, our hosts had morning chores to complete, but they insisted we rest by the fire.

Col thanked them while Magnus finished his ale and then picked some of the food off Col's abandoned plate.

When the farmers left, I continued to glare at the prince. "Tell me more," I said.

Col came to sit beside me, bringing a chair with him and placing it by the fire. This time, Magnus joined him. "Col..." he began.

Col shook his head. "Not until she understands." Then he looked at me. "The package that you and I have sought these last few weeks, once in the wrong hands, can be used for great destruction. As you know, my goal was to get it before The Harrow did. There are several smaller kingdoms that The Harrow is currently trying to gobble up, like the pig that he is. I have no intention of letting him use a weapon to destroy masses of people at the same time.

"You've been a great help to me, Samara, perhaps without even knowing how much." Col smiled sadly. "How many days I wasted with you, when they could have been spent in your arms."

My cheeks flushed, this time truly from embarrassment because Magnus was sitting right there and heard everything. I cleared my throat.

"I don't know what this package is," Magnus said, "but The Harrow is calling for you to show yourself, Col. To show yourself or... he will kill every person left in your kingdom."

A chill ran down my spine, and I shivered despite the fire.

Col didn't react much, other than to tighten his jaw. "That doesn't make any sense. Last I heard, The Harrow was basically enslaving everyone in Iron Deep, putting them to his own uses."

Magnus shrugged. "And as you know, The Harrow is not a sane man. He doesn't care about losing slaves if it means he can get a hold of you. And it seems he's finally decided to make it happen. Here's the rest of it—he says that if you don't show yourself, he will kill everyone in the entire kingdom in one night. I have no idea how he'll do that, but—"

Col and I exchanged a knowing look, and Magnus frowned.

"We know how he plans to do it," Col said, looking at me thoughtfully. "But we also know that he does not actually have this weapon in his possession, perhaps not quite yet, though it could be on its way to him this very minute. It's more important than ever that we find it before it can be used. And we have very good reason to think it was here only two days ago."

"What is this abomination?" Magnus asked.

Col lowered his voice and told him what it was, and Magnus's eyebrows shot up under his shaggy, golden hair.

"Samara and I had thought we lost the trail," Col continued, "but now we know exactly where it's headed —to my kingdom."

CHAPTER EIGHTEEN

*M*agnus stood. "Tell me where your things are, and I'll fetch them. I'll go with you, and I know the rest of the seven will, as well."

A thrill ran through me at knowing once again where the alicorn horn was headed, and yet, I felt more awkward than ever. And who were the seven Magnus spoke of?

"We can arrange for you to stay here with the farmer and his family," Col said to me. "Or somewhere better if you prefer."

"You're not going to even ask if I want to go?" I asked. "You asked me not to walk away, yet you are doing that very thing to me."

Magnus looked down at his boots, which suddenly seemed very interesting, and Col frowned. "It has become more dangerous than ever to be with me. Perhaps I've already put you in more danger than I should have, though I truly didn't want to. This is going to come down to a fight, and though I'm going to do my best to keep it from happening, I could very well die. I don't want to ask you to take on that danger."

"Magnus said he would, though, and that's okay?" I said, standing. I had never seen a man the size of Magnus try to look less conspicuous.

"Magnus knows the risks," Col said, his voice even. "Magnus can fight."

"So he is useful to you. And now that you got what you want from me, I'm not longer useful."

"That's not what I'm saying at all," Col said calmly, holding my gaze. "The way ahead could mean any number of things for me, and I don't wish any of them on you. But, if by some chance I'm successful, I can come back for you, or I can summon you and have you brought to me."

"If?" I asked, shaking my head. "So I'll just wait here like a good little woman while you go to your possible death. That sounds like great fun, truly. Thank you, Col, for making this easier for me."

"Easier?" he asked warily.

I straightened my shoulders and stared at him, and as I made up my mind, the broken pieces of my heart were blown away by the wind. I didn't think I'd ever get them back.

"My sister and father need me, and I've left them alone far too long. I have to go home."

Col looked as if I had punched him.

Turning away from him was the hardest thing I had ever done, but I didn't look back as I left the house to get my things from the barn.

Col followed me, and I tried to ignore him as the

goats greeted us. When I looked up into the hayloft, a burning shame coursed through me. Shame for what happened there, not because it hadn't been beautiful, but because I had let him in, and I knew better.

Much to my irritation, Col followed me up the ladder. He watched me pack, but I refused to look at him, to meet his eyes. I didn't want him to know how hard he was making this. Then I remembered something and grabbed the dagger he had given me, tossing it toward him.

But Col pushed it back toward me. "Keep it. And..." I half hoped he would ask me to reconsider, that he would beg me to stay with him.

He didn't. It was just as well.

I nodded my thanks, grabbed my things, and climbed down the ladder. Col followed me with his own things.

When we left the barn, Magnus was standing there with three horses. I had no idea where he got them from, if they had already been close by, or if not, how he had suddenly found them. He reserved a tall, gray horse for Col, who hopped into the saddle as if he had been born there. And then I realized he likely had, growing up as a prince.

Magnus kept the large black horse he'd brought for himself, and held out the reins of the smallest horse for me. "This mare should get you home," Magnus said matter-of-factly, but not unkindly.

I took the reins, and though the horse put her ears back and tossed her head, she didn't try to bolt.

"Samara," Col said.

I looked up at him finally, still half hoping he would

get down off that horse and beg, and I knew right then that if he did, or if he grabbed my arm and whisked me behind him onto the saddle, that I would go with him.

Yet it was right for me to go home, and the thought of it made my heart break in a whole new way. Flint wouldn't be there. Neither would Col, of course. I hadn't gotten the alicorn horn for myself, and now I never would. I would be empty-handed. But I had paid my debt, and it was time to go.

"I hope to see you again someday," Col said finally. Then he held out a small bag of coins, probably all he had left. But then he was a prince—he could get more, right? "Be safe," he said.

I couldn't take the money, couldn't even look at it. Instead, Col dropped it to the ground and then turned his horse, and I watched as he and Magnus rode west.

Straight into the heart of war.

I sobbed, tears rolling down my cheeks as I realized I would never see Col again. I ignored the coins on the ground. They felt like payment for something, and I wasn't about to accept, not after what happened. It made me feel cheap, usable.

But I had nothing. Anger, shame, and sorrow all claimed a piece of me as I snatched up the pouch and tucked it into my belt. Not for me, but for Laney. I couldn't leave money on the ground, on principle.

Before Col and Magnus were even out of sight, I tied the new horse nearby, and went back into the house to get my cloak.

Then, I would leave all of this behind me. I was going home.

THANK YOU

Thank you for taking a chance on me and reading *Of Exile and Song*. If you enjoyed the book, please leave a review and then sign up for my mailing list at tiffany-huntromance.com/newsletter to have deleted scenes from this book sent to your email (as a thank you).

I love these characters and have thoroughly enjoyed getting to tell their story. Book 2 is in progress, and is about 80% complete as of this publication. I will send out an email as soon as it is available for preorder. Until next time.

ACKNOWLEDGMENTS

I would be remiss if I didn't acknowledge the people who helped bring this book about. First, thank you Claire for the beautiful art. Your work is exquisite.

Thanks to Merwie for the great editing and insightful comments. (Any mistakes are mine and not hers.)

And thanks to Fictive Designs for working to bring my world into being through their map illustration, and Etheric Tales for the beautiful heading and break illustrations.

Thank you to the ARC team for taking a chance on a new series and unknown author!

And last but certainly not least, thank you to my family, who puts up with me stopping conversations to make random story notes. I love you.

ABOUT THE AUTHOR

Tiffany Hunt writes all things fantasy romance with salty characters, action, kick-butt heroines, and spice. If it has castles, magic, and hunky, irresistible men (or elves, etc), she's down for it.

Her favorite tropes are enemies-to-lovers, one bed, fake dating, arranged marriages, and forbidden love.

Sign up for newsletter updates (only new releases) at tiffanyhuntromance.com.

facebook.com/tiffanyhuntromance

instagram.com/tiffanyhuntromance

tiktok.com/@tiffanyhuntspicy

ALSO BY TIFFANY HUNT

Of Exile and Song

Of Kings and Thieves - Coming Summer 2023

Printed in Great Britain
by Amazon